THE ICE CHIPS AND THE MAGICAL RINK

THE ICE CHIPS AND THE MAGICAL RINK

Roy MacGregor
and Kerry MacGregor

HarperCollins*Publishers*Ltd

The Ice Chips and the Magical Rink
Text copyright © 2018 by Roy MacGregor and Kerry MacGregor.
Illustrations copyright © 2018 by Kim Smith.
All rights reserved.

Published by HarperCollins Publishers Ltd

First edition

HarperCollins books may be purchased for educational, business,
or sales promotional use through our Special Markets Department.

HarperCollins Publishers Ltd
2 Bloor Street East, 20th Floor
Toronto, Ontario, Canada
M4W 1A8

www.harpercollins.ca

Library and Archives Canada Cataloguing in Publication
information is available upon request.

ISBN 978-1-44345-228-1

Printed and bound in the United States
LSC/H 9 8 7 6

To every kid's first skate.
—Roy MacGregor and Kerry MacGregor

For Sarah, who introduced me to hockey.
—Kim Smith

THE ICE CHIPS AND THE MAGICAL RINK

CHAPTER 1
Location Unknown

This can't be real!

I HAVE to be dreaming!

Lucas Finnigan brushed his right forearm over his eyes. His eyelids felt as if they'd been glued together. He couldn't see a thing.

The snow was swirling now, the wind whipping it across the field and straight into his eyes, where the flakes stuck and melted, blurring his vision.

Where was he? And where was Edge? And Swift?

Both of Lucas's teammates from the Riverton Ice Chips had been with him only moments ago—*hadn't they?*—as they'd started across this field to get to ... where?

No, wait—

This field ... it wasn't here before. We were on ice, weren't we? Skating ...

It had to be a dream. Lucas had no idea where he was or how he even got here.

He took a step and felt an awkward crunch, like a blade

scraping a rock. He looked down and saw that he was wearing his skates. They were half-covered in snow. Lucas was standing in a small, flattened-down patch, almost like the imprint of a snow angel, where bits of soil were poking through. No footprints led to the patch and no footprints led away from it.

It was as though Lucas had landed here . . . *like some kind of alien spaceship.*

He shivered. *Impossible.*

Lucas looked down at his hands, confused. His stick was here, too. The stick he was holding *had* to be his. Number 97—that was *his* number.

He twisted off his hockey glove and used his shivering index finger to clear the snow off his wrist comm-band—the small walkie-talkie worn by each kid on his hockey team. Lucas first said "17," for Edge's jersey number, into the band. The comm-band picked up a signal, but all Lucas could hear was blowing snow. Then he tried "33," for Swift. Again, the sound of wind or of someone moving—then emptiness. *Where are they?*

Lucas brushed his eyes again and stared at his comm-band. Was it broken? Was the snowstorm interfering with the radio signals? For a moment, a red message flashed across the tiny screen:

"NO SIGNAL!"

And then the comm-band went black and restarted itself.

Suddenly, the wind died with a sigh. It was as if this world—wherever it was—had run out of breath. Lucas could finally see as the swirling snow looped once and settled to the ground.

He looked around. Off in the distance were two horses wearing red blankets and kicking at the snow. Steam rose off their backs like pots simmering on the stove. The horses whinnied and moved on, kicking more snow in search of grass to graze on.

Lucas was in a field, probably a farmer's field. It seemed to stretch on forever. The storm clouds were breaking up now, and shafts of sunlight almost as blinding as the snowflakes were breaking through. Behind the vanishing clouds, the sky seemed . . . *too big*.

He called out for Swift and Edge—but nothing.

Up ahead, Lucas could see that the field dipped down into what looked like a surface of polished steel—shiny and grey, like the top of a table he'd once seen in a hospital. He moved toward it, carefully stepping one skate and then the other into the freshly fallen snow, gripping his stick tightly as he went.

Lucas worked his way down the slope. Then he stepped out onto the steel surface—and his feet flew out from under him, sending him crashing onto his back! Fortunately, his head was cushioned by the thick snow along the edge.

It's ice! Now Lucas knew he had to be imagining this. *It's a rink! And it's . . . outside!*

Both his mother and his father had often talked about winters when they were very young and how Riverton's lake used to freeze over. Lucas's grandfather—he called him Bompa—had shown him some faded pictures of kids playing hockey on what looked like the biggest rink in the world. But Lucas had never done it.

That's what this is, he thought, breathing in the cold air. A frozen river. Or a small lake. And the wind had cleaned the ice as surely as if a Zamboni had been at work. The ice was thick and hard—hard enough to skate on.

Lucas pulled himself up so he was sitting on the snowbank that surrounded the rink. He looked across the ice, marvelling at its existence . . . and at the fact that he was the only one there to see it.

Where are Swift and Edge?

Have they vanished? Are they in some . . . other world? Or in danger?

Just then, two figures appeared over the crest of the snowy slope with the sun behind them. Lucas squinted: he saw a spray of snow kicked up by a boot and heard voices—voices he didn't recognize.

And they were coming toward him!

CHAPTER 2

Lucas wiped his eyes again. He could see the two strangers swinging their arms and lifting their knees as they worked their way through the deep snow. As they drew closer, he noticed they were wearing thick, funny-looking coats, like the ones in Bompa's old photos, and had knitted toques pulled over their ears. The girl's toque was a bright, bright red, and the boy's was grey. The girl had a burlap bag slung over her shoulder, and both were carrying what looked like hockey sticks.

Lucas dropped his stick, unsure of what he should do next.

The kids were now almost at the pond, laughing as they half-fell down a steeper slope to the ice surface. Lucas didn't think they'd seen him yet, but he wasn't sure . . .

Should I hide?

They were just kids, but Lucas still didn't know where he was—*where he'd landed.*

Quickly, he scrambled a few feet away from the ice

and ducked down behind a snowdrift that had built up against some small trees. He was breathing quietly, trying to stay low, when suddenly—

BZZZZ-SHEEEP-ZZZZ!

Lucas's heart nearly jumped out of his chest. Edge was calling him! NOW!

But from where?

Panicked, Lucas quickly turned his comm-band off. It was too loud . . . too risky. Had the strangers heard it? What would they do if they found him?

He tried to stay calm.

The two kids were now on the ice, getting ready to skate—but each of them had only *one* skate! The girl had taken a skate from her burlap bag and put it on her right foot, but her left foot was still in a green rubber boot with a grey sock sticking out the top. The boy had done the opposite: he had a skate on his left foot and a similar rubber boot on his right. Both kids looked awkward. Even with their thick socks, the skates were far too big for them.

But they were trying. With their mismatched footwear, they hopped and glided, hopped and glided. There was something different about their hockey sticks, too, Lucas noticed. They were made of wood and they were flat, as if they'd been cut straight out of a thick piece of plywood with a cookie cutter—all one piece.

How can they hoist a puck without a curve in their blades?

And what was that . . . *puck* they had? It looked even weirder than the sticks.

With their strange equipment and single skates, the boy and girl stopped in front of the snowdrift where Lucas was hiding, both dragging their rubber boots as brakes. The girl was smiling. The boy, taller, had his mouth open in a big grin.

They *had* seen him, Lucas realized. It could have been the buzz from the comm-band—or maybe they'd seen him all along.

"Hi!" the girl said, looking over the snow and stepping off the ice. The boy followed. "I'm Edna. This is Gordon, my little brother."

He doesn't look so little, Lucas thought as he stood up. The boy seemed so shy he couldn't speak—or even look Lucas in the eye when he was being introduced.

"I'm Lucas." He brushed the snow off his coat.

"We don't know you," Edna said, without any meanness. "Where you from?"

"I'm . . . uh, visiting . . . my aunt and uncle." Lucas figured he should change the subject quickly, before she asked for a name. He looked down. "Don't you have a regular puck?"

The boy blinked. "No . . . we use . . . road apples." He spoke with long, awkward pauses.

"What's a road apple?" Lucas asked. "An apple that fell off a delivery truck?"

Gordon turned and pointed back to the horses, still kicking the snow in search of grass.

"Ha, ha. Not quite. Our *pucks* . . . fall . . . out of their butts."

Edna giggled. Lucas looked from the road apple to the horses, from the horses to the road apple—and got it. *If it weren't so cold*, he thought, *I could probably smell this puck.* But if it weren't so cold, the horse manure likely wouldn't hold together. The idea was gross, but Lucas couldn't help but giggle, too. His little brother, Connor, would have found the idea of a frozen poop puck hilarious.

"I've got a real puck for you," Lucas offered, taking off his hockey gloves.

He checked the pocket of his coat—he almost always had a puck on him. But the only thing he found was his lucky quarter. It was an old commemorative one that Bompa had given to him, from the 2002 Winter Olympics. It reminded him of the lucky loonie that had been placed under the ice that year, when Canada's men's and women's hockey teams had both won gold. His quarter was for the men's team, and on it was a hockey player skating in front of a dark red maple leaf with his stick held high in celebration. It was Lucas's lucky charm.

Still searching for a puck, Lucas plunged his hand into his other pocket.

This one was filled with Cheerios! Connor must have put them there. His little brother was wild about

Cheerios. The Cheerios spilled out of Lucas's pocket and onto the snow.

Edna, Gordon, and Lucas all reached down to grab the tiny cereal rings, so none of them noticed when Edge and Swift arrived at the top of the snowy slope on their right and began to climb down in their skates. Nor did they notice the two other hockey players who were just stepping onto the ice on the other side of the pond—two mean-looking boys with thick, dark sweaters and scowls on their faces.

"What're they?" Edna asked Lucas, holding a few pieces of cereal in her hand.

"Cheerios," Lucas answered, distracted. He was still wondering where his puck had gone.

Gordon blinked.

"What're . . . Cheerios?"

CHAPTER 3
Riverton

Lucas Finnigan was hunched over his puck, smiling. He was focused, he was ready . . . and he was about to make the perfect shot.

Lucas paused for a moment and then, quick as lightning, pulled back his stick and fired—

Smack!

Squooosh!

"Wooo-hooo!" cheered Lucas's little brother, Connor, from across the kitchen table. A soggy Cheerio had landed just above Connor's left eyebrow, fired there by the curved blade—well, actually, spoon—of his older brother.

"Again!" Connor squealed. A drop of milk slid down the curly-haired toddler's cheek and landed on the tray of his high chair. He opened his mouth wide and shut his eyes.

Ever since he was Connor's age, Lucas had turned everything imaginable into a hockey game. He wore hockey pyjamas, slept with hockey sheets, and always went with a hockey theme for Halloween (even though

last year's puck costume hadn't made it to the end of the night). Lucas also shot Cheerios the way Wayne Gretzky fired pucks—or at least that's what Connor thought.

On the ice, the "top shelf" Lucas aimed for was the highest area inside the hockey net, just above the goalie's shoulders and below the bar. During breakfast, his "top shelf" was Connor's screeching, laughing, wide-open mouth.

"'GAINNNN!" Connor screeched as Lucas drew back his spoon and lobbed another shot.

Connor beamed as Lucas's Cheerio flew by him and the one from his forehead fell onto his hand. He shook it off so it squished onto the side of the fridge, where it stuck like a magnet to the glossy photograph of Lucas's hockey team.

Lucas moved quickly to wipe away the wet cereal.

He treasured this picture of the Riverton Ice Chips, all posed together on the ice of their beloved rink. Lucas was right in the middle, beside his best friend, Ekamjeet Singh— or "Edge" to everyone on the team. Edge had made a joke and Lucas had laughed just as the photo was snapped. In it, his thick brown hair seemed to spring out of the holes in his helmet and his pudgy baby face was smiling from ear to ear. He looked hilarious and he loved it.

At the time the photo was taken, Lucas suddenly realized, he still thought that he was going to make it to the National Hockey League—that he'd play with the pros, win the Hart Memorial Trophy, and bring the Stanley Cup back to his hometown.

But not *now*.

Now Lucas was almost sure he'd never make the NHL.

He wasn't even sure he'd make it through novice—not with the way he would look on the ice this year.

"Loo-KASS! Aaaaa-GAIN!" Connor cried, but their mother shushed him so she could hear the radio in the kitchen.

An advertisement for Henry Blitz's new sports complex was playing. Mr. Blitz was the richest man in town, as well as the coach of the Riverton Stars, the other competitive novice team. Apparently, his new high-tech complex was going to include a synthetic rink—a plastic "ice" surface—and all its lights could be controlled with a phone. The radio ad made the building sound unbelievably futuristic, almost like it belonged on another planet.

The Stars were moving to the new complex this year, leaving the Ice Chips by themselves at the Riverton Community Arena with their beloved coach, George Small. Lucas was glad. The community arena, his dad often joked, was the Ice Chips' second home. The Stars and the Ice Chips would still hold tryouts together, as they did every year, but now they each had a practice space all their own.

And today was the beginning of it all: those tryouts would start right after school.

Normally, Lucas looked forward to them, but this year, his stomach felt tight—*nervous*.

So much had changed . . .

Lucas had grown taller—quite a bit taller. At school, he was now as tall as most of the boys in the next grade up. He was skinnier but also stronger; he could skate faster, and his reach was longer. His mom had even cut his hair shorter with a razor, which looked cool. The problem? He could no longer fit into his old equipment.

Lucas needed new gear. Badly. And he wasn't getting any.

His family just couldn't afford it.

Six months ago, Mrs. Finnigan had opened her own store, the Whatsit Shop. It sold things that people couldn't find anywhere else. The store's motto was "Bits and bobs for the oddest jobs." Then, just after the Whatsit Shop opened, Lucas's dad had lost his job as a mechanic. Reluctantly, he'd gone to work at the store as well.

Now the boys' parents were always busy, always rushing—especially in the mornings—and always worried about money. Lucas didn't understand it all, but it was obvious to *everyone* that life in the Finnigan house had changed.

Even Lucas's oldest cousin, Speedy Finnigan, knew it.

Just before the start of the school year, Speedy had quietly dropped off a worn hockey bag filled with his old equipment. None of it fit quite right and all of it stunk, but it was all Lucas had. He'd have to make do.

Lucas shook off the thoughts of his reeking hockey

gear and leaned across the kitchen table, ready to fire a few more breakfast pucks at his little brother.

"That's enough, boys," their mother called from the hallway as she tossed Lucas's lunch into his backpack.

"Don't you still have some homework to do? Your journal?" Lucas's father reminded him from the living room. He'd been digging toys out from under the couch with a hockey mini-stick and rushing around with the vacuum.

"Nope, it's done," Lucas said proudly, holding up the picture he'd been working on between cereal shots. Each day, he drew one of hockey's greats for his journal entry: Connor McDavid, Steve Yzerman, Gordie Howe . . . But today, he'd decided to draw a player who wasn't so great: himself.

At least I can have new equipment in a drawing, Lucas was thinking, feeling sorry for himself, when his comm-band suddenly buzzed.

He ignored it. It would just be Edge, who was *always* up early, calling so they could walk to school together. Edge's mom had given all the Ice Chips comm-bands as a gift last season, but Edge was definitely the one who used his the most.

BZZZZZZZZZZZZ! BZZZZZ!

Lucas rolled his eyes. "Edge, come on! I'm still in my pyjamas!" he said under his breath, making Connor laugh. Connor was still in his pyjamas, too. His mother had just released him from his high chair, so now he was running around the living room.

Connor giggled as he wobbled over to the front door and back again.

BZZZZ-SHEEEP-ZZZZ!

This time, the buzz sounded right in Lucas's face — Connor was holding the comm-band up under his chin.

Reluctantly, Lucas said, "Hello, comm," and the wristband crackled to life. He'd barely finished answering when the shouting began.

"You gotta get here fast!" Edge yelled through the comm. "I'm already at the school with Swift and Crunch!

"We got an emergency!"

CHAPTER 4

As fast as Lucas could, he threw on some clothes, pulled his backpack over his shoulder, and took off running out of the house.

Edge never had emergencies. He had big ideas, and he drove Lucas nuts with his made-up words—especially when he called Lucas's old skates *blade-onators*—but Edge never made up stories.

This *had* to be real.

As Lucas raced down Elm Street and turned right on Montreal Road, he could see Edge waiting up ahead, at the playground beside the school. He was with Nica Bertrand, known as "Swift" to the team, and Sebastián Strong, the Ice Chips' math nut, known as "Crunch."

Lucas started running even faster to meet them—*What could have happened? What??*—but then his eyes suddenly grew wide . . . He raised his arms to his head and dove to the ground.

ffffffff-WHOOOOOOSH!!

Lucas somersaulted twice in the grass before coming to a stop, his backpack flying off and the lunch his mother had packed spilling out and breaking apart.

ffffffff-WHOOOOOOSH!!

Again a powerful breeze blew past him, scattering more dirt onto the sandwiches that had fallen into the gutter.

Lucas looked up. It was a plastic drone the size of a Frisbee, its lights flashing. It seemed to rock uncertainly in front of Lucas and then it shot off again into the sky, clipping the branches of a nearby oak tree as it rose.

With leaves falling all around him—some of them already turned the colour of fall—Lucas began picking up his lunch and putting his sandwiches back together. Maybe he could wash the dirt off; maybe he'd just go without.

"Those sandwiches looked gross anyway!"

It was Lars Larsson, a new kid at school. He was on the other side of the street with a remote control in his hands, smiling. Lars pushed a button and the drone did two more awkward loops before falling sideways into the grass near Lucas's feet.

"*Loser!*" Lars chuckled as he breezed past Lucas and bounded into the thick, wild grass to recover his toy.

Lucas had seen Lars hanging out at school with the Blitz twins, Beatrice and Jared—the spoiled kids of Mr. Blitz, the owner of the new rink complex.

Of course any new friend of the Blitz twins would pick on Lucas. He wasn't sure why, but the twins had never liked him — not since kindergarten, and definitely not when they met him on the ice, whenever the Ice Chips played the Stars. No one had even gone through tryouts yet, and already the twins were wearing new team jackets with crisp maroon and gold stars over their hearts and their names stitched across the arms. Lucas was surprised Lars didn't have one, too.

"Bea says you're a forward, like me." Lars chuckled mysteriously as he walked out of the grass with his drone.

Bea? wondered Lucas. *Not even Jared calls Beatrice "Bea."*

Edge was now waving from the playground.

Confused, Lucas nodded toward Lars. It was true. He *was* a forward. Why should he hide it?

"Then I guess you're more like a 'backward' now that you've got nowhere to skate! Right?" Lars laughed, happy that his joke had been set up perfectly.

But his laugh was too loud, too mean . . . and Lucas didn't get it.

What is he talking about?

Another kid on his way to school, Dylan Chung, came down the path. Dylan normally talked and talked when they were in class. But at this moment, he said nothing. Once Dylan had seen Lars, he'd just hurried past with his eyes to the ground.

Lucas was zipping up his backpack, ready to go, but he could already feel it coming on — down, down, down in the very pit of his stomach, where it could churn and burn.

The fear.

There was nothing Lucas hated more than being picked on. It was worse than his fear of the dentist, his fear of needles, even his fear of swimming at his grandparents' cottage after someone had pointed out a giant snapping turtle. This fear was different because he didn't know what to do about it. He didn't know how to make it stop.

"At least you're not the *only* loser on the team, right? Now you're all losers!" Lars laughed. His white-blond bangs had fallen over his eyes, but Lucas could see he had a smirk on his face. He was still waiting for Lucas to react.

But Lucas didn't, which seemed to make this new kid even madder.

With a smug curl of his lip, Lars suddenly swung his backpack over his shoulder and started off toward the school—as though he'd made his point anyway and his work there was done.

Lars *was* just like the Blitzes, who Lucas thought had a cruel streak, both off and on the ice. But at least on the ice, referees could deal with sneaky trips and lippy talk. Off the ice, Lucas was on his own.

Well, partly.

"There you are, Top Shelf!" Edge yelled, calling Lucas by his team name as he made his way up the hill. Edge was making his voice extra loud on purpose, so Lars could hear him from across the road.

Of course, Lars didn't even turn around.

Edge continued running toward Lucas, with Swift and Crunch close behind him. Crunch had his computer tablet tucked under his arm. Swift's long strawberry-blonde ponytail had slipped out while she ran, so she was tying it back up again with an elastic. They were all out of breath.

"Why would he say we're *all* losers?" Lucas asked once Lars was far enough down the road. *Is this why Edge was buzzing my comm-band so frantically?*

Edge closed his eyes. He didn't want to say it, but he couldn't keep it in. "Lucas, our rink is being closed."

Lucas blinked twice and his mouth fell open.

"*What??* Who's closing our rink?"

Is hockey being cancelled? What about the Ice Chips? Is this some sick joke?

"Seriously," said Crunch, who was always serious. He coughed uncomfortably and adjusted his glasses. "Edge isn't joking."

"Crunch read us the story in the paper," Edge said sadly, motioning toward the tablet, which Crunch then handed to Lucas.

Lucas read as quickly as he could: "Mayor Abigail Ward told council that due to a lack of available parts, the town would be unable to repair the Riverton Community Arena. The Riverton rink . . . is to be immediately shut down."

"Available parts? For *what*?" Lucas asked in shock, handing the tablet back as they walked.

"My dad said the problem is in the refrigeration room, where they keep the chillers for the rink," said Swift. Her dad was an engineer with the city, and he often helped out at the arena. He'd explained that the special liquid that usually flowed through the pipes underneath the arena floor was no longer freezing the rink—the pump that was supposed to push it through the pipes wasn't working right. And there was a problem with one of the chillers. That didn't look good either, because the machine was old and parts were hard to find. Swift's dad said they needed a rare fuse and a certain size of belt, and no one had them. "That's one reason why they're making one of Mr. Blitz's new rinks out of synthetic ice—it's just easier."

"Easier? What it *is* is c*rud-o-stupid*," Edge said in disbelief. He looked over at Swift, urging her to tell more.

"My dad helped shut everything down last night around suppertime," she said sadly. "And my sister, Sadie . . . she even had her figure skating practice on Mr. Blitz's synthetic rink this morning. She said she hated it."

"That's not even real ice time," Edge said angrily. They all felt cheated.

But Lucas wasn't giving up that easily.

He spoke slowly, his voice catching in his throat: "But on *our* rink . . . the ice surface is still there, right? Our ice hasn't melted yet?" He was desperate, searching.

Crunch looked at the time on his comm-band. "By my calculation, that's . . . thirteen hours and twenty minutes with no freezing. It could still be . . ."

"Wait, what're you—" Edge turned toward Lucas just as the school bell cut him off.

As they all hurried toward the doors of the school, Lucas whispered as quietly as he could. He didn't want anyone to hear him—especially Lars up ahead—but a plan, if they were going to have a plan, had to be made *now*.

"We've got to skate it. We have to, if they're shutting it down," Lucas said. His eyes were pleading. He was almost shaking. "One last skate on our home ice . . . yeah?"

Crunch nodded and Edge gave Lucas a quick pat on the back. They were in. Whatever Lucas was suggesting, they were in.

Swift almost had tears in her eyes as she turned back toward them. "You're right. We're going to have to break in—*tonight*."

CHAPTER 5

By sunset, Lucas and Edge were crouched in the bushes beside the main doors of the Riverton Community Arena, waiting for Swift's buzz.

"She'll do it. She'll get us in," said Lucas, pushing his blue hockey bag closer to the wall, trying to hide it in the shadows.

Now all they had to do was wait—and listen.

There was a chilly wind blowing through the maple trees in the parking lot. The sun had just gone down, but Lucas could still see the branches moving in the darkness. Somewhere far away, a motorcycle was driving by, and those gentle creaks, the drawn-out clicks, were probably crickets off in the dist—

"Gotcha!" a voice called out behind them as the sound of footsteps—clumsy, eager footsteps—rounded the building.

Lucas jumped back and fell over his hockey bag.

Edge just laughed.

Crunch.

"You guys had *better* become hockey players when you grow up—you definitely can't be spies!" Crunch giggled. He had on an old-man-style wool hat with earflaps, perched too high on his head, and was clutching a lumpy garbage bag to his chest.

Edge quickly grabbed him by the elbow and pulled him down into the bushes.

"Shhhhhh!" Lucas warned.

"Yeah, I know—*shhhhhhh*," Crunch said without embarrassment as he tried to tuck himself under one of the taller bushes in the small, dimly lit rock garden.

Lucas noticed a hole in Crunch's garbage bag where a skate blade had broken through. With a smile, he carefully touched the tip of his friend's protruding skate. *Crunch always has weird ideas*, Lucas thought affectionately. "Being Crunchy" was what Edge liked to call it. All of Crunch's family members were the same. They were all really smart but wacky, like absent-minded professors— even Crunch's little sisters, who spoke four languages, including Spanish like their parents.

"I told my mom I was taking the garbage out and—" Crunch whispered proudly, but Edge quickly threw his hand over his friend's mouth. He had heard the click of the arena's front doors.

Someone was coming out!

"It's fine. It's going to be fine. You shouldn't worry." The tall, grey-haired man who had come out of the arena

was speaking nervously into his cellphone. It was Quiet Dave the Iceman, as the kids called him—the friendly but soft-spoken man who cleaned the ice.

With the rink closed, Lucas had almost expected the arena to be boarded up. He had definitely expected the rink's caretaker to be gone.

"Ace, this is my last chance," Dave pleaded as he turned his key in the front doors and locked them.

They called him Quiet Dave, but Dave wasn't being so quiet tonight. Lucas had never seen him so worked up. In fact, he couldn't remember the Iceman ever talking much at all. The kids would say hi and Dave would nod. Coach Small would thank him for cleaning the rink and Dave would say, "Yep." Their Iceman was sort of like a farmer, Lucas guessed, or anyone who was used to working in a big space all alone.

"I know you don't agree with me," Dave continued loudly, looking around to make sure no one was listening, "but I have to do this."

In the bushes, Edge now had his arms out in what Swift called his "superhero mode," as if he was guarding his two teammates or holding them back.

Ever since Lucas had started hockey, he'd known Dave. The guy was probably sixty years old, and he had looked after the rink forever. In the last few years, small patches of grey had appeared on the sides of Dave's hair, but he still had a childlike grin on his face whenever he watched the Ice Chips play. Sometimes Lucas even felt that the Iceman wished he were out there with them.

Is Dave ... mad about retiring?

Lucas checked the time on his comm-band. *Swift should be here by now.*

"We need him to leave," Crunch mouthed to his teammates.

And then, as though he had heard Crunch's plea, that's exactly what Dave did.

"Look, I forgot a part anyway, and I can't go without it," he said as he pulled twice on the door to make sure it was secure. "I have to go home and get it. I'll be about an hour. Yes—it's locked. The place has been shut down anyway. No one will be here."

Dave's voice trailed off as he headed angrily into the parking lot, still clutching his phone to his ear. "Look, Ace, if you're coming, meet me here. If you're not ... well, then I'll do it without you."

Suddenly, the three Ice Chips' comms buzzed.

And the lock on the doors turned again, only slowly— and this time, from the inside.

❖ ❖ ❖

"I thought he'd never leave!" Swift bellowed as the front doors of the Riverton Community Arena swung open with a loud click.

The first part of the plan had been on Swift: she'd rushed home after school to grab her dad's extra set of rink keys before he got back from work. Since the rink was closed, they'd figured no one would notice if Swift "borrowed" the keys from his desk drawer.

"I came in through the Zamboni entrance," she said proudly, acting like she owned the place. Except for her skates and goalie pads, she was already dressed for a game.

"Hey, not so loud!" Crunch pleaded as he stepped inside. But with Dave gone—at least for an hour—the coast was finally clear.

Edge was looking around the entrance of the arena, grinning. He loved this kind of adventure. "*Magna-mazing!*" he said. "Lucas is right. We can't let go of this rink."

"Well, wait until you see the ice," Swift said, still at full volume. She turned toward the rink. "Oh, and my sister's here. She caught me taking the keys . . . but I don't think she'll be staying."

"Why not?" asked Lucas as he slung his hockey bag over his shoulder. He liked Sadie. She didn't play hockey, but the risks she took on the ice, leaping and spinning from one skate to the other, were always impressive.

"Like I said, wait until you see the ice," Swift called sadly, disappearing into the arena.

Lucas moved as quickly as he could toward the Ice Chips' dressing room, and Edge and Crunch followed. He had brought his full gear, but Edge had only brought his skates, helmet, shin pads, and a big pair of mittens. They were two very different players anyway: Lucas's equipment was all well worn and didn't fit right; Edge's equipment was as high tech and as new as it could get.

On game days, Edge was always the first ready, and Lucas was always the last. Even now that Edge had started wearing his patka—the cloth often worn by Sikh boys over their hair—at the base of his helmet when he played, he still dressed faster than Lucas. On days when they had to go straight from school to the rink, Edge could unwrap his hair from the bun on top, move it to a wrapped ponytail in the back, and get into all his equipment before Lucas had even tightened his second shin pad. Maybe that was because Lucas couldn't go out on the ice without retaping his blade perfectly—usually twice, just to get it right.

Edge *liked* hockey, but Lucas *loved* it.

Sometimes Edge even felt guilty that *he* was the one whose dad had once been a professional athlete. Whenever anyone asked who his "hockey" heroes were, he sometimes even said Dhyan Chand and Sandeep Singh, two famous players from India's men's national field hockey team—his dad's old team. Edge thought both sports were "*outstan-delicious.*"

Without stopping, Lucas pushed open the heavy dressing room doors and let them swing closed behind him.

"Wait—*what*?" Edge called out nervously. "Tops, what about the trophy case?"

It was Lucas's ritual: before entering the dressing room, he'd stop at the dusty trophy case in the hall, kiss two fingers on his right hand, and press them against the glass where a picture of the District Championship Cup was displayed. In the faded old photograph, a dozen sweaty-faced players were grouped together on the ice as two smiling ten-year-olds in the middle held a heavy, shiny trophy above their heads.

"One day, those two kids will be us," Lucas was constantly telling Edge.

Once he'd moved past the trophy case, Lucas would run his hand along the ledge of the skate-sharpening shop and then straighten an old wooden picture frame that hung beside it. He'd straighten the frame even if the black-and-white picture of old skates was straight to begin with. *Every practice, every game.*

All the Ice Chips knew this—especially Edge, who didn't believe in superstitions.

But today, Lucas hadn't stopped.

With the closing of their rink, Edge suddenly realized, not even Lucas thought his superstitions could save them.

CHAPTER 6

"Hey . . . *let's GO!*" Swift's voice echoed off the boards.

She opened and closed her glove a few times and then bent down on the ice in front of the net, pushing her goalie pads apart. She leaned left to stretch, then right. And each time she stretched, her strawberry-blonde ponytail almost touched the ice—the surface that had softened and was now covered in thin, shiny puddles.

But so what?

Now that she was on the ice, Swift was convinced the rink was skateable. *Mostly.* At least, she knew *she* was skating on it.

Why wasn't anyone else?

While Swift had let in the boys, her sister had managed to turn on half the rink's lights. But now Sadie—who was often grumpy, and slightly wild—was sitting in the stands in her skates, with her elbows on her knees and her head in the palms of her hands, staring at the rink.

"This is worse than the plastic ice!" she yelled. "And that means it's terrible!"

"Come here and say that!" Swift shouted with a smile, trying to push Sadie into stepping onto the ice. She knew her sister couldn't resist a good fake fight.

But Sadie scrunched up her mouth and shook her head. "I'm not going anywhere near you—*or* those puddles!"

Swift was getting anxious: Crunch was now sitting in the stands with his garbage bag, poking at the screen of his tablet, but where were Edge and Lucas?

Like Lucas, Swift took the game of hockey very seriously. A lot of training and a lot of commitment had gone into getting her onto this team—onto this ice.

When Swift was five years old, she'd become very sick with meningitis. The doctors had told her parents that they might have to replace the bottom part of her leg with a robotic one. And in the end, they had.

In her hockey equipment, no one could tell the difference between Swift's two legs—and that wasn't only because both skates had purple laces. Swift was an amazing athlete, on either foot. The other Ice Chips were convinced that she would eventually compete at the Paralympics— probably in more than one sport.

"Forget about the water. *Sadie*, let's see what you can do!" Swift called from the crease, slapping her stick down into a puddle for emphasis—just as Edge and Lucas emerged from the dressing room.

Edge, Lucas . . .

. . . *and Lars.*

* * *

"If *you* can skate here, *I* can skate here," Lars threatened, pushing his way ahead of Lucas and Edge, as though he wanted to beat them onto the ice.

Edge moved as if he was going to run after him in his skates, but then didn't. They'd been arguing ever since Lars had walked into the dressing room. How had he known they'd be there? Why had he come out? And why wouldn't he just leave them alone?

Swift couldn't believe it. Neither could Crunch. And Sadie didn't know what was going on.

Did Lars actually think he was going to skate with them?

The look on Lars's face was angry . . . mean. But once he reached the stands where Crunch and Sadie were sitting, he suddenly turned around and burst out laughing— at Lucas.

From the waist down, Lucas had dressed in full hockey gear, but as soon as he'd seen Lars enter the dressing room, he'd decided to keep his coat on up top. He hadn't wanted this mean new kid to see Speedy's ketchup-stained jersey (at first Lucas had thought it was blood—but no) or his over-sized shoulder pads (he hadn't even put them on). Lucas was already embarrassed. He didn't need Lars telling him he was a loser who was never going to make it to the NHL.

"Hey, Lucas, *you* stink. I mean . . . you actually *stink*," Lars howled, pointing at Lucas's lower half—Speedy's old gear. "And that is the *wooooooooorst* ice I've ever *seen!*" Lars's voice boomed across the arena. He pretended to steady himself against the boards, laughing far louder than necessary. "No wonder they're closing your rink!" he sneered, his raised eyebrows hiding behind his bangs.

Lucas looked out across the ice, deflated. Edge, who was always optimistic, was disappointed, too.

"This isn't how I thought it'd be," Lucas said under his breath.

"You *can* skate on it," said Swift, now leaning in the open doorway of the boards. "You just don't want to take any dives—or else you'll go for a swim."

That was it for Sadie. In one quick movement, she grabbed the skates she'd just taken off and put them back in her skate bag. "Well, *I'm* not going swimming. I'm going home," she said, hopping down out of the stands. "I'm sorry"—she looked at her sister sympathetically—"but this was a bad idea."

"An *awful* idea," said Lars with an annoying grin.

All the Ice Chips instantly wished that they'd thought to lock the rink's doors behind them.

"Why don't you take Lars with you?" Edge said to Sadie. "He obviously doesn't want to be here."

Like Edge, Lars was still in his street clothes. All he had to do was change back into his boots.

"First, I want *Top Shehhhhhlf* to take off his coat so we can see the rest of his gear," said Lars.

Lucas's face burned red. This was mortifying . . . and time was running out.

"I'll take *my* coat off," Edge offered, coming to Lucas's defence. He removed his puffy green coat and placed it on the stands. "I wasn't going to skate with it anyway."

"So you can go home now, *Lars*," Swift quickly added.

"How about we shoot for it?" Lars suggested in a tone that was almost diabolical.

What is with this guy? Lucas couldn't believe it.

He could tell that Lars wasn't even planning on skating now. He just wanted to make Lucas suffer.

"Me . . . and *Lucas*," Lars continued as he twirled his stick in his hand. "A shootout."

Lucas winced as Lars nodded toward a large blue steel door in one corner of the arena. *The chiller room.*

"If you hit the doorknob, I'll leave," he said with a mocking smile. "If *I* hit it, you carry my equipment for a *week*—all the way to the new rink."

Lucas looked at the doorknob. He had practised that shot, the one that hit right below the top of the net, a million times over the summer.

But what if he couldn't do it?

CHAPTER 7

With a thud, Lars dropped an orange ball from his back-pack onto the rubber floor, right in front of Lucas's skates.

"This is silly," said Swift, pushing off the boards and then drifting back again. "No one can hit that."

Crunch slid his tablet aside and said he was going to look for a broom "to push the puddles around." Sadie rolled her eyes and took another step toward the Zamboni doors.

"What? Are you afraid his awful equipment will *fall off* when he shoots?" Lars said with a taunting grin. "Wait—what's that sound? Are your shin pads . . . chattering?"

Lucas looked at the ball but didn't move.

Swift pulled herself along boards to where Lucas was standing. Always protective of his friend, Edge moved in closer, too.

"All you have to do is hit the *doorknob*," Lars repeated smugly.

"ARE YOU KIDDING ME?!" Edge shouted, butting in with his biggest voice as he fiddled with his helmet. "That's not even a *real target*."

Edge loved coming to the rescue.

He means well, thought Lucas, *but his acting is terrible*.

With an exaggerated motion, Edge put his hands on his hips like his mom did when she asked about his homework. "You want him to hit *that*? Really? No problem, Lars! No problem *at all*."

Lucas would have found this amusing if he hadn't been so terrified.

"Okay, but not with a ball," he said, swallowing hard. "I need a puck."

Lucas pushed the orange ball away with his skate and took a puck out of his pocket—the one he'd thrown in there, along with his lucky quarter, just before leaving the house. With a slap, he dropped the puck on the rubber flooring.

All at once, the room went silent.

Swift, Edge, Sadie, and Lars were staring at Lucas's stick. Crunch was still off looking for a broom.

"Would you hurry up!" called Swift, still worried about their skating time.

Lucas lined up the puck.

He drew back his stick.

And without leaving himself time to hesitate, he fired.

Shhhhhh-cah-LACK!

The puck lifted slightly off the ground. It flew fast, in a straight line, and then turned slightly just as it slammed into the metal doorknob.

BOOOO-ooooom!

Gaad-OOOOOong!!!

The loud metallic sound exploded across the arena.

He'd done it!

And it was like nothing any of them had heard before. The sound was way louder than the smack of a puck against a metal garage door. It made a bigger boom than Sidney Crosby's shots off the clothes dryer in his parents' basement. (They'd seen a video on the internet.) It was . . . *incredible*, like big, empty metallic thunder.

"*BOOM-errific!*" Edge cheered as he patted Lucas on the back.

The vibrations were still hanging in the air as Lars sat down and started unlacing his skates.

No one was surprised that by the time Crunch had come back around the corner from his broom search, a sour-faced Lars was already in his boots, headed for the door.

"Lars isn't going to shoot?" Crunch asked, confused.

Lucas just smiled and shrugged. "And you're leaving, too?" he asked Sadie.

"The puddles are too much for me," she answered heavily, still clutching her skate bag. The melting ice might not be dangerous for hockey, she said, but she didn't want to swing around for a Salchow jump, slip, and break a leg—she wasn't *that much* of a risk-taker.

"Well, *I'm* still skating," Swift said impatiently, looking at Crunch as Sadie bounced toward the Zamboni exit and left. "Did you find a broom?"

"Not exactly," Crunch replied, holding out his hands. In them was an old, rusted remote control with strange buttons and a flashing green light. "I, uh . . ." he said, glancing over at the main doors to make sure they had closed firmly behind Lars.

Swift motioned for him to go on.

Carefully, Crunch cleared his throat. "I think I found something a little more . . . interesting."

CHAPTER 8

"NO WAY!!!!"

None of the Ice Chips could believe it when Crunch showed it to them—the remote-controlled machine that was now cleaning the ice. It was only the size of a ride-on lawnmower, and it looked like someone had assembled it out of spare parts—an old air duct here, a used bike part there—but the job it was doing was . . . magnificent!

The Chips had never seen anything like it.

As the machine swerved around the rink, crossing through the middle and then veering left or right with the curve of the boards, it almost seemed to be floating over the ice. But at the same time, it was also *part of* the ice. Was that even possible?

Lucas watched in awe from behind the boards as the little flooding robot scratched the surface, glided over it, and smoothed it out. Not a single puddle was left behind.

It was *amazing*.

"It's a puddle eraser!" Edge shouted, impressed. "It's like a . . . *supra* . . . *glass-ificating*—ugh! I mean, the ice is like new!!"

Lucas let out a little giggle.

But Edge was right.

Wherever the machine had passed, the ice was now unbelievable—solid, flawless, and glossy like a carefully glazed mirror. Their regular Zamboni had never done anything like *this* before.

When Crunch had first shown the Chips the remote control in his hands, Lucas had assumed he'd found another drone—maybe the first one ever invented, from the look of it. But then Crunch had flicked the orange switch on the top of the controller, and something magical had happened. Something . . . *special*.

Lucas had sensed it, like a shiver going through his entire body.

The moment the switch was flipped, he'd felt something electrical.

"*Whooooa*, what *is* that?!" Swift had shouted as the boards swung open and the rusty blue-and-white machine rolled onto the ice. Its lights were blinking excitedly, almost like a dog wagging its tail, and Swift spun quickly on her blades and bolted.

"It's amazing!" cheered Crunch as he let Swift through the boards.

"It looks like some kind of pet," Edge said, laughing.

Then *he* stepped his skates onto the ice, daring to take a closer look at the strange contraption. It had one small seat and a steering wheel on top, but it obviously didn't require a driver. "It's so tiny. What's it for?" asked Edge, leaning in. The name "Scratch" had been carved into the machine's side and painted blue. Edge reached out his hand to touch it and—

Suddenly, the machine lurched forward!

Edge jumped back. Could it be dangerous? Could it . . . bite?

Frightened, Edge, too, quickly skated off the ice.

At first, Scratch had chugged along by himself, his large back wheels gripping the ice beneath him, spraying water from two large containers on his back. But the ice had stayed the same. That's when Crunch realized that Scratch didn't have a towel attached to the track on his back bumper—the towel that smooths the ice after a flooding machine drives over it.

If that was what Scratch really was . . . *but what else could he be?*

With only twenty minutes left before Dave was supposed to be back, Swift immediately marched over to the change room and grabbed her towel and Lucas's from their bags. Edge and Crunch then fastened them to the machine.

Now, as Scratch made his rounds, line after line, with the towels attached, he had Lucas mesmerized—absolutely, completely transfixed.

Lucas's heart was fluttering.

His hands were sweaty.

Even the idea of his rotten equipment seemed to have faded into the distance.

As Scratch finally finished his half ovals and rolled back down the Zamboni chute all on his own, Lucas couldn't stop grinning. He had never seen a sheet of ice so stunning. His beloved rink was now flat and even, shimmering in the big overhead lights.

It was absolute perfection.

* * *

In the hockey world, there is nothing quite so lovely as a clean sheet of ice.

Sometimes, that first step — that first stride — was Lucas's favourite part of the game. The rink has been flooded. The game can begin. No one knows who will shine, who will succeed, who will fail, who will triumph.

Coach Small often talked to the Chips about character: telling them that who they were on the ice was made up of both the opportunities they saw and the ones they created. Lucas wasn't quite sure what that meant, but he knew he'd never seen an opportunity like this one.

"It's perfect . . . *the best ever*," he said, breathless, as the Zamboni gate closed behind the flooding machine.

Perfect — and empty.

Lucas and his friends could smell the ice. They could almost taste it.

Their rink was calling them.

* * *

The players decided that Lucas would be the first to touch his blades to the clean white surface.

Then Edge. Then Swift.

Crunch wasn't going to put his skates on at all. If their rink could be like this—this *changed*, this awesome— then they'd have to work harder to keep it. Mayor Ward, Crunch was convinced, would never shut this rink down if she knew what it could do. Someone would have to film "the phenomenon," as he called it.

"I'll start with a wide shot, then I'll come down to ice level for some close-ups," Crunch chattered excitedly as he crawled back into the stands. "But I'm warning you now—if Dave comes back, I'm running."

Crunch was always afraid of getting in trouble, but he could often find some extra courage when Lucas and Edge were involved. He held his tablet up to eye level and started recording.

"Okay, *action!*"

Slowly, Lucas put one skate onto the untouched surface—afraid to scratch it, but dying to at the same time— and then the other.

"Lucas, *go!*" said Swift, giving him a nudge. She was itching to get back on the ice.

Breathing in the icy air, Lucas pushed off the boards. *And flew.*

Shhhhhhhhwuuuuh.

Shhhhhwoooooooo.

Weightless, he shifted from one leg to the other. He moved his stick back and forth with an imaginary puck. Skating on the perfectly groomed ice was like floating. No, like . . . *flying.*

When Lucas reached the goal line, he cut hard and stopped, angling his skates tight together. A small, perfect spray of ice shot out beside him.

"*This is AMAZING!!*" Edge shouted as he bounded onto the ice after Lucas, pushed hard with his legs, and roared up behind him. Edge was gripping a stick with one mitten and held a puck in the other, as though he was weighing it, judging it.

"It's . . . wow. It's *unbelievable!*" Swift agreed as she skated in beside them. "It's like a completely different rink."

"An Olympic one," Lucas whispered under his breath as he moved his skates back and forth, feeling the hardness of the ice.

"Do we give the rink a moment of silence?" asked Edge with a giggle. He always found solemn moments like this funny and awkward. He never knew what to do.

"No . . . let's race!" Swift called out as she took off skating—backwards—toward the blue line. "First one across centre wins!"

Lucas leaped after her. A moment later, so did Edge.

Lucas and Edge would be quicker than Swift in her goalie pads, but she had a head start.

Swift hit the blue line first and turned sharply, almost losing her balance. From there, she skated forward.

Lucas drove his back leg out hard, pushing with all his strength. He was crouched down now, skating the way he'd once seen Bobby Orr skate in an old video—almost as if he were pulling a chair up to the breakfast table. He pushed out hard with his right leg, then, gliding on his right skate, pushed hard again with his left.

Edge was doing the same, only faster.

Edge, Swift, and Lucas all hit the centre red line at exactly the same moment . . .

. . . and vanished.

CHAPTER 9
Location Unknown

This can't be a dream, Lucas thought to himself. *It can't.*

Snow doesn't really fall in dreams. It doesn't stick your eyelids together. You don't slip on the ice and fall backwards with a *whuuumpppp* and then still feel sore later . . .

"You don't have a puck, then?" Edna asked. She and Gordon were still wearing one skate and one boot each, but now they were also holding a few Cheerios.

"It's here somewhere," Lucas answered, kicking at some cereal in the snow. Then he remembered — he'd shot it in the arena . . . before . . . *before . . .*

What happened?

There'd been a flicker of light.

A swirling motion.

Snow, maybe snowflakes. Cold.

Then in a flash, the rink had looked sideways, upside down . . . and bright, bright white. Brighter than anything Lucas had ever seen . . .

And then it was gone.

"What's *under* this?" someone called from the frozen pond.

Swift—Swift and Edge!

Lucas, Edna, and Gordon turned to see the two Ice Chips moving slowly toward them along the pond with their sticks in their hands and their heads bowed. Lucas knew that they couldn't believe what they were skating on!

"The ice . . . is still a little . . . bumpy," Gordon said apologetically, thinking he was answering Swift's question.

Lucas noticed that Gordon had turned as red and bright as his sister's toque. And he wasn't looking at Swift as he spoke.

Swift was in her hockey equipment, Ice Chips jersey and all, but Edge didn't even have a jacket on—just a thick long-sleeved shirt, his helmet, and some wool mittens. He looked frozen.

"This is amazing," said Edge, still looking down. Slowly, he opened and closed his skates, tracing a caterpillar pattern below. Then he rubbed his mittens together and stuffed his hands into his armpits. "I could get used to this . . . well, except for the cold."

"Hi!" Swift said as she brought her skates together and stopped between Lucas and Edna. "I'm Swift. This is Edge."

"Hi, I'm Edna. Your names are cute as a bug's ear," she said with a giggle.

"I'm . . . Gordon." Her tall brother smiled shyly.

"You wanted a puck? I got one," said Edge as he pulled a thick black disk out of his back pocket and turned it over in his frozen mitten. His skin was now red from the cold. Lucas felt bad for him. "It was in my hand when I . . . I guess . . . um, *here*." Confused, Edge flipped the puck onto the ice, where it landed with a slap.

Lucas realized that Edge's brain had to be as scrambled as his.

"Yes!" shouted Gordon. "If we can borrow your puck . . . you can borrow my jacket—I've got a sweater underneath . . . like Swift's. I won't be cold."

Gordon slipped off his jacket to reveal a well-worn wool sweater—maroon with thick white stripes knitted into the sleeves. It wasn't at all like Swift's. There was some kind of logo on the front, but it was so battered, Lucas couldn't make it out. On the back, the bottom of the number 9 had ripped off and some of the stitches at the top were coming loose. But Gordon didn't seem to care. He was proud of it.

"Thanks," said Edge, slipping into Gordon's jacket. The arms were too long, but that didn't matter. At least it was warm. "The puck's all yours."

With a big grin, Gordon immediately swatted the puck with his stick. Then, running lopsided with both feet, he lifted his boot, slid on his one skate, and chased after it.

"Why only one skate?" Edge asked Edna.

Edna laughed. "A neighbour sold our mom a bunch of

hand-me-down clothing and these old skates—she needed money for milk. We fought over them, and he got one and I got the other. I told Gordon I'd sell mine to him for a quarter—but he doesn't have that kind of money."

A quarter? thought Lucas. *Who doesn't have a quarter?*

"We tried calling you," Swift said quietly to Lucas. She glanced at Edna and then at the two unfriendly looking players clearing off their patch of ice farther down the pond. Carefully, she pulled up her sleeve. "But our comm-bands reset themselves. They weren't working, although I think they're okay now."

"What're they?" asked Edna. "Watches?"

"Hello, comm," Lucas said.

His comm-band lit up and then fizzled. Then slowly, it came back to life.

"Maybe it's the weather?" Lucas said, bewildered. "Now I've got a signal." But he didn't really mean the weather. He meant the big snow globe that had landed them here—or whatever it was that had shaken them up and then dropped them in the snow. *Should I try calling Crunch? Is it even possible to call home?*

"'Signal'?" asked Edna. "What on earth are you talking about?"

Their chatter was interrupted by a puck smacking into Swift's goalie pad. The four kids turned and looked to see where it had come from. Far down the ice was Gordon, grinning.

"He didn't hoist that all that way!" said an incredulous Lucas.

"Who else?" asked Edge. "He's the only one shooting at us."

Gordon hobbled and slid on his one skate back to the gang. "Sorry about that," he said, deeply flushed. "I been . . . working on my strength—maybe too much. I been . . . pulling myself up like this on the barn . . . door frame." Gordon held his hockey stick above his head and pretended to do a chin-up.

Swift let out a laugh.

"I didn't mean to," said Gordon, looking down at the ice again. "I'm . . . really, really sorry."

"He doesn't know his own strength," said Edna. "He's always doing things like that. I should give him this other skate so he can really play."

"You said I had to . . . buy it," said Gordon. "I don't . . . have a quarter."

Lucas took a deep breath. He had a quarter. It was his lucky coin, but here was something that Lucas knew he should do. All the poor kid wanted was a second skate so he could actually learn to use them.

Lucas dug back into his pocket and pulled out his cherished Olympic keepsake. "Here," he said, handing it to Edna. "Give your brother the other skate."

Edna took the coin and looked at it, both sides, then handed it back to Lucas.

"He can have the skate," she said. "But I don't want your quarter—who knows *how* you got that much money. You're just a kid."

"I didn't steal it," protested Lucas, taking the quarter back. This time he noticed it felt different. It felt heavier.

"Well, you never know," said Edna as she hopped and slid over to her brother.

Lucas ran his thumb along his quarter as he always did. But that felt different, too.

He looked down at the coin and then immediately held it out for Swift and Edge to see.

Instead of a hockey player skating in front of a red maple leaf, Lucas had been running his thumb over the raised picture of a man's face. He had a giant moustache and a crown, and was looking off into the distance. The words around his head weren't even in English!

Lucas flipped the coin over, and all three of the Ice Chips gasped.

The quarter, which had been made to honour the gold medal win at the 2002 Olympics, had been completely transformed.

On the tails side, it now had a wreath of maple leaves following the curve of the coin.

And the date.

1936.

CHAPTER 10
Canadian Prairies

1936?!

Lucas rubbed his eyes again—this time, in absolute puzzled wonder. He looked at Swift, who also seemed in shock. They both looked at Edge, who seemed to be pinching himself.

"Look!" said Swift, pointing.

Across the field, beyond the steaming horses still searching for grass under the snow, was an ancient black truck moving along the road. It was the sort of vehicle the Chips had seen at the car show in Riverton, where old-fashioned cars and trucks from all over the country were put on display each summer.

Another black truck was going the other way. And a third one was now passing a horse pulling some kind of wooden box with four big wheels—it had to be a horse and buggy! This was no car show. This was . . . *the past.*

And it was happening right now!

"Look at the skates," Edge whispered to his two teammates.

Edna was pulling her skate off her foot while Gordon was pulling the green rubber boot off his. Gordon tossed his boot into a snowbank, near the burlap bag Edna had been carrying.

"Toss me my other boot," Edna said, pointing over at her bag. "We'll use yours as goalposts."

Gordon was ecstatic. "I'll owe you a dime, at least," he said, grinning as the boot he'd thrown toward Edna landed right beside her socked foot.

Edna now had two rubber boots and Gordon two skates.

Lucas had never seen skates like that. The blade was completely different than anything he knew. It looked like a tube or something, and the boot of the skate looked soft, like a leather shoe. It didn't even have the hard ankle support of Speedy's old Bauers.

Gordon was lacing up his new skate as fast as his fingers could move. He stood, uneasily, and edged out onto the ice—and promptly fell flat on his bum!

Edna was laughing, but Gordon was determined. He got up, wobbled a bit, and then fell again.

Lucas's skates, the old ones from Speedy, looked lame in comparison to Edge's and Swift's but fabulous compared to the old skates Gordon was trying to master.

Gordon's skates seemed hopeless.

"Does he not know how to skate?" Swift asked.

Edna shook her head.

"Well, we've got ours on," Edge said. "Let's show him how."

"Yeah!" Swift agreed enthusiastically, just as Gordon bailed again, almost bumping his chin on the ice. Lucas felt relieved that the two players clearing their own ice farther down the pond hadn't seen it. He wasn't sure why, but he felt protective of Gordon. He liked him.

"Good luck," said Edna with a hopeful smile.

❊ ❊ ❊

"Gordon just asked me how we can see the puck with these things on our heads," Lucas whispered warily to Edge as their new friend made another wobbly circle around the ice. "He means our helmets—no one had helmets back then . . . uh, I mean *back now*."

"They didn't have many Sikhs around here either in 1936, I bet," said Edge, smiling and touching his mitten to his helmet. "But it's cold out and we don't have toques anyway. As long as they don't think we're plastic-headed spacemen, let's keep them on."

Swift was now skating slowly beside Gordon, trying to give him some coaching and encouragement. Lucas and Edge circled around to give them a little room.

Edge pushed out from the shore and glided away from Lucas, flexing his ankles from side to side almost as if he were skiing. The movement had the effect of sending him down the ice without either blade ever leaving the surface. It was an easy trick, and Edge liked to start each practice or game with a bit of it.

Lucas, feeling the wind on his face, turned and headed the other way. He flew down the ice with the wind at his back, sweeping past Gordon, still knock-kneed and wobbling, before coming to a hard stop that sent a high spray of snowy ice into the air.

The ice felt different. It was . . . *harder*. That struck Lucas as ridiculous. Ice was ice. Wasn't it? All ice should be the same—unless it was melting. But this wasn't at all like the ice in the indoor rink back home. This was ice so hard he could feel his blades dig in the moment he switched to real skating. And there was a sound as he skated.

A sound almost like bacon frying in a pan.

A sizzle.

This was amazing!

With Lucas on one arm and Swift on the other, Gordon was able to take his first few strides on the ice. Lucas was amazed at how thick the kid's arm was. He felt strong. Strong as a man.

Lucas encouraged Gordon to copy Edge's stride—he was, after all, one of the best skaters on the Chips—and Gordon caught on quickly, heading down the ice all on his own and then trying a turn with a sharp stop like Lucas had done.

Gordon's legs flew out from under him and he crashed down hard on his side. But he was laughing. He was loving it.

The two other players down the ice—the ones in the thick dark sweaters who seemed to be scowling—looked over. They were laughing in a different way, but then went back to what they were doing. They'd finished sweeping the snow off the small section of ice where they were going to play, and they were lacing up their skates.

"Look at Gordon's blades," Edge said. "He needs a sharpen."

Lucas looked and saw rust all along the bottom of the blades. No wonder he couldn't turn and stop. They'd have to get them sharpened . . . but where?

Edna had a suggestion. She knew a man who sharpened saws and knives by hand. He came around to all the houses and farms each summer in a wagon—chiming a bell that told people the "sharpener" was there—but in winter you had to go to his place.

"I'd love to see that," said Lucas, "but I guess I'd need boots." He was already worried that he'd scratched his own blades on that rock in the field. His skates probably needed a sharpen, too.

"Well, you're in luck," said Edna.

She tossed Gordon his boots from the snowbank—they hadn't made their goalposts yet—and then walked over to her burlap bag and undid the leather strap.

"These came from our neighbour, too," said Edna, yanking out a third pair of green rubber boots. "Our brother Victor was supposed to be here today at the slough."

Victor had probably gone off with the other boys to watch the trains come into the station, she explained, since the Ceepee Bridge over the North Saskatchewan River had recently been finished.

"He's just got shoes . . . with a hole in one sole," said Gordon as he slipped off one skate, then the other, and reached for his boots. "We were going . . . to surprise him."

"Wait—what's a *slough*?" Lucas asked, confused. *Haven't we been skating on a pond?*

"This," said Edna, pointing at the icy surface. "The Hudson Bay Slough."

"The what?"

"It's good for animals. So they can get a drink. Don't you have animals?"

"I have a cat and a dog and a brother," said Lucas.

Edna rolled her eyes and laughed.

"I'm sorry we don't have more . . . boots," Gordon said to Swift and Edge, who were now passing the puck back and forth over the bumpy ice surface. Lucas could tell they were happy to stay behind.

Edna turned to Lucas and pulled her knitted toque down over her ears with a smile. "We'd better get walking."

CHAPTER 11

Skates off, the gang of three began walking along the road into the town. Lucas noticed that only a few of the homes had vehicles in the driveways or on the street. Were people all at work? Or were they poor? At one corner, they came across the strangest thing: a *car* being pulled by a team of horses. Not a buggy this time, an actual car—with its motor turned off!

"A Bennett buggy," Edna told him when he asked what it was. "Don't you have them where you're from? They're named after our useless old prime minister, our dad says. He's gone now, but the people without jobs still can't afford gas. Some had to go back to using horses."

"Times are tough around here," Gordon added quietly.

They came to a corner house that had a wagon but no horses. The wagon had a sign on the side: "Ward's Sharpening." It was filled with snow.

An older man with more hair in his ears and nose than on his head came to the door, listened to their story, and invited them in.

"Grampa! It's a party! We're having a party!" a little kid squealed as he ran into the front hall. He wanted to greet their guests, too. The boy was four or five years old and was running around with a pair of underwear on his head—despite the fact that he was fully dressed.

Lucas and his friends had to stifle their giggles.

"That's my grandson, Robert," the old man said with a chuckle. "He fancies himself an inventor."

"Today I'm a soldier. And this is my helmet," Robert said loudly, watching them through one of the leg holes. "But I've been fighting all day and I'm hungry!"

The old man grabbed some dried apple slices from a jar in the kitchen and gave them to Robert. Then he took the skates, put heavy coats on himself and his grandson, and stepped out into the garage. The kids all followed.

Lucas wondered where the man's sharpening wheel was. He loved how the stone wheel would start spinning with just a flick of a switch. The skate would be locked into its holder, and then there would follow the most beautiful sight and sound Lucas had ever known—the sparks flying off a blade as the sharpener smoothly worked the skate along the spinning wheel.

But there was no such machine. And no switch, either. It was dark in the shed—there weren't any windows. The old man removed what looked like a bottomless glass vase from the top of a heavy, metal-topped glass jar filled with yellow liquid. Then he lit a match and touched it to a piece of cloth sticking out of the metal lid. The cloth, which was soaking in the yellow liquid below, burst into a large flame that the man made smaller by turning a tiny metal wheel. He then put the glass vase back over top, and to Lucas's surprise, the whole room took on the small flame's glow.

Mr. Ward took a file and began working along the blades by hand. He used several files to remove the rust and then took a flat, rounded stone into his hand. He spit twice on the stone and began rubbing it along the grooves of each blade.

Edna and Gordon had moved to the other side of the skate sharpener, closer to the garage door where they could watch, but Lucas was happy beside Little Robert—that's what Edna and Gordon had called the grandson. The boy reminded him of Connor, only skinnier.

Besides, Lucas had decided he shouldn't get his own skates sharpened after all—he couldn't risk an adult figuring out they were from the future.

"You play hockey?" asked Little Robert, swinging his legs on the old trunk where he was seated. He had pushed his underwear toward the back of his head and was now wearing it like a toque.

Lucas nodded. For him, hockey was the only game that existed. To prove it, he quietly opened his coat and took his thin school journal from his inside pocket. He'd stuffed it in there when Lars had unexpectedly walked into the Ice Chips' change room—so Lars couldn't grab it and make fun of him.

Lucas turned to the page where he'd drawn himself—the Lucas he wished he could be this year—dressed in all-new equipment.

"What *is he*?" asked Robert, gently taking the journal from Lucas's hands.

"It's a hockey player. The kind they'll have when you're a grandpa . . . maybe . . . I mean—" He didn't know if it was safe to tell anyone their secret—even a little kid.

"Wow, that's aces!" said Robert, grinning from ear to ear. "Wanna see what I *drawed*?"

Robert gave the journal back then pulled a folded piece of paper out of the back pocket of his too-big jeans and opened it up. It looked like a kid's blueprint for some kind of machine, one with wires and buttons, but Lucas had no idea what it was supposed to be.

"It's my invention," Robert said excitedly.

"Now, Robert," said Mr. Ward, smiling in Lucas's direction. He'd just stepped back to take a look at his work. Gordon's blades were shining now that the rust was gone. In the light of the strange lamp, which was casting monster-like shadows of him and Edna on the wall opposite, they almost sparkled.

Mr. Ward handed the skates back to Gordon.

"How much?" Gordon asked.

"Nothing," Mr. Ward said. "I know who you are. Your family can't afford it."

Gordon smiled, but Lucas could tell he was embarrassed.

"Do you want to see something really swell before you go?" Robert whispered to Lucas while Gordon carefully tied his skate laces together.

"Sure," said Lucas.

Robert reached up to one of his grandfather's worktables and picked up a thin, stretchy square of material. He stretched it lengthwise and widthwise, and then pressed the material up against his nose as if he were looking through a screen door.

"The material's 'ny-lon.' My American friend just invented it," Mr. Ward said somewhat proudly. "Sent it in the mail. Says one day it'll be in ladies' fashion or parachutes—not sure which. But it's interesting."

"We're going to make inventions out of it—*like this one!*" Robert cheered. He leaped off the trunk and quickly opened its lid.

Inside was something that looked like an old sewing machine, but there was a sharpening stone attached to the part where the needle would normally go. There was a piece from a film projector and part of . . . Lucas didn't know what. Nothing matched, but somehow the odd parts seemed to fit together.

"It's me and my grampa's invention," said Robert excitedly, pointing at the drawing he'd done and showing how it matched up with the bizarre machine in front of them. "See? The *ny-lon* is the *belt*."

At first, Lucas couldn't figure out what he was seeing.

Then Robert's grandfather pushed a button on the machine, and a light attached to an old car battery went on. Two wheels started turning slowly, with what looked like a pair of nylons wrapped tightly around them—the belt. The wheels turned some gears that moved the sharpening stone, but then the machine suddenly fizzled and stopped.

"It's not . . . finished." Mr. Ward shrugged without seeming embarrassed.

Is this really the first skate-sharpening machine? Lucas couldn't help but be impressed.

* * *

As they were leaving the sharpener's house, Lucas's comm-band suddenly buzzed.

"Hello, comm," he said quietly into his wrist, but the call was gone.

Gordon and Edna exchanged looks but didn't say anything.

It had been Swift.

Lucas immediately buzzed her back.

The reception was fuzzy and he could make out only a few words: "You'd better get back here."

CHAPTER 12

Even before the three kids arrived back at the frozen slough, they could hear the distinctive, unmistakable sounds of hockey being played. There was the lovely *click-click-click* of someone stickhandling, the rasp of skaters stopping fast, the yelling and cheering that said something special had happened.

Gordon seemed very nervous as they approached the outdoor rink. He stayed a few steps behind Edna, almost like he was trying to hide.

The two grumpy-looking players who had arrived at the rink at the same time as Edge and Swift were still there, but now they had friends. And they'd taken over the part of the ice where Lucas and his teammates had been teaching Gordon to skate.

Is this what Swift meant—that they'd been pushed out?

"Maybe we should . . . get home, Edna," Gordon said to his sister. "We can come back . . . tomorrow."

"Don't be silly," Edna told him.

Soon, they reached Swift and Edge, who were on their own, rolling over the bumpy strip of ice they'd been left with.

"See? We've got enough players here for our own team if we want," Edna said cheerily. "I'll play goal—you don't need skates for that."

"You can borrow my goalie pads," said Swift with a smile. She didn't mind being an out player for today.

Gordon seemed unconvinced. But he wasn't going to argue with his older sister.

The five moved over to the snowbank so Gordon and Lucas could put on their skates. There were five other kids there—the ones who'd taken over their ice—all in hockey equipment, all chasing the same puck. They had set up their own green rubber boots as goalposts for a net. It was pure shinny—every player out for him- or herself.

When the kids playing saw that the others had arrived and were lacing up, they stopped and stared. One of the players—the biggest boy, with a frown on his face that made him look like the bossiest, nastiest kid imaginable— skated straight over fast and stopped so quickly and hard that the spray from his skates covered Edna and Gordon with snow.

"Well, well," the kid said in a mean voice, "if it isn't the 'road apple' gang. You still passing hunks of manure to each other?"

"We have a puck now," said Edna, brandishing the one that Edge had given them.

"Where'dya get them skates, Doughhead?" the kid asked Gordon.

Gordon had his boots off but was still proudly wearing the newly sharpened blades around his neck like a medal. "None of your . . . business," he answered, taking his skates down and setting them on the ice in front of him.

"Doughhead-Doughhead-*Doughhead*," the big kid teased. "Doughhead can't even look at me!"

"Leave him alone!" Edna shouted. She seemed about to take a swing at the kid, who wiggled back on his skates and started laughing.

"Doughhead'll never make a hockey player. He can't even learn *school*, for one thing. The only kid in town who's flunking grade three!"

The four others with the mean kid were also laughing, though none seemed to enjoy the teasing as much as the kid doing it. Lucas wanted to wash the guy's face with snow.

"Can you even skate, Doughhead?"

"He's a good skater," Lucas blurted out. He surprised himself by saying anything.

"Who the heck are you?" the bully kid demanded.

"They're our friends," said Edna. "They're just visiting for the day."

"From *where*? Mars?" The kid was sizing up their bizarre equipment.

Lucas put his helmet back on and stood up on his skates, making himself taller. He dusted off Speedy's old hockey pants without even thinking about how worn they were.

"Wanna get your butts whipped?" the kid asked, scowling and laughing at the same time.

"You're on," said Swift. "First team to score five goals wins."

"Wins what?" the kid asked.

"I don't know. You tell us," said Edge.

"If my side wins," the kid said with a snarl, "Doughhead here has to carry my hockey stuff home for me. He's always doing push-ups and silly exercises at school—carrying my stuff is exercise, so I'll just be helping him out."

Lucas felt his teeth grinding. He'd heard that kind of deal before. It was exactly what Lars had tried to do to him back in Riverton. This big kid was out to humiliate Gordon. What a bully!

"Let's do it," a voice spoke out clearly.

Lucas turned. It was Gordon, standing at his full height—even taller than Lucas—and no longer staring at the ground. He looked absolutely determined.

CHAPTER 13

"Who is that nasty kid?" Lucas asked as the five were getting ready.

"Yeah, he's being a crank-o-saurus," added Edge.

"Tommy Boland," said Edna, who had strapped on Swift's goalie pads as best she could. "School bully. Total jerk. He's a good hockey player, though—says that he's already got junior teams after him, and that he'll be the first player from this town to make the NHL. He's probably right, but no one likes him."

"They seem to," Edge said, nodding at the other four.

"More likely they're afraid of him." Edna shrugged. "They all live on his street. He runs it like a gang."

"What's that 'Doughhead' thing all about?" Lucas asked.

Edna sighed, turning her right goalie pad a little. She wasn't quite sure how it was supposed to fit. "Gordon has trouble at school. He doesn't learn well—but he's smart. He just learns differently. You saw it yourself with the skating."

She grabbed her stick and slid across the ice in her own boots with Victor's under her arm. These she set apart to make "posts" for their goal, just as the others had done.

"No raisers," Edna called to the other side. "These goalie pads probably don't work too good—they're skinny."

"No raisers," Tommy snarled back as he raised his elbows behind him.

"Faceoff," said Edge, reaching down to pick up the puck. He moved to roughly halfway between the two makeshift goals on the frozen slough and held out his hand with the puck in it.

Tommy skated up to where Edge was, his skates snow-plowing to a stop and his stick on the ice.

"What about the national anthem?" Lucas asked, thinking he was making a little joke as he got into position opposite Tommy.

"No 'God Save the King' here," Tommy said with a sneer. "It should be 'God Save the Doughhead'!" He howled with laughter at his own joke.

"God Save the King"? Lucas wondered. *What's that?* Canada's national anthem was "O Canada." He shrugged, accepting that there were things around this frozen slough that made no sense to him whatsoever.

Edge dropped the puck and Tommy immediately bowled over Lucas with his shoulder, taking the puck and skating back into his own end.

"No hitting!" Edna screamed from her net.

"An accident!" Tommy shouted back, smirking to himself.

Lucas got back to his feet, brushed the snow off his pants, and started after Tommy. He was skating fast and easily, and his speed surprised Tommy, who decided to pass the puck off to one of his teammates—only to have Swift come out of nowhere, pluck the puck out of the air, and stickhandle it down the ice.

Before Swift played goal for the Ice Chips, she used to play out in the middle with Lucas and Edge. It had been a long time since she'd been out like this, skating with the puck, but she still remembered a few tricks.

Swift dropped the puck back into her skates, kicked it forward as she swooped around the last player's back, and neatly released it between the goaltender's legs, the puck sliding through the rubber boots and on down the ice.

1–0.

Now the other side came charging again. One of them, the girl, was a good stickhandler but a slow skater. Still, she made it past Edge's check and slipped the puck over to Tommy, who fired as hard as he could at Edna, just missing her arm.

"Hey, no lifters!" Edna cried.

"Accident," said Tommy, not even bothering to hide his satisfied smile.

1–1.

Back and forth went the action on the frozen slough. The fresh, cold air made Lucas's cheeks turn red until he could no longer feel them or his nose. Yet the sweat was trickling down his back and soaking into his shirt.

Gordon was something to behold. The kid who had stood so clumsily on rusted blades earlier in the day now had the skating stride down perfectly and was moving effortlessly over the ice. He had his stick down, and Lucas hit him with a perfect pass. Gordon took a quick shot that went into the corner of the goal to put his side ahead.

And then Tommy crashed into him.

The bully came across the ice and blindsided Gordon, smashing his full shoulder into the younger boy's chest and side and sending him crashing to the ground. Gordon's head hit the ice with a sharp crack. It sounded like a rifle had gone off.

"Hey, sorry there, Doughy—I didn't see you," said Tommy, leaning to help Gordon back up. "Accident, eh? Sorry."

Lucas had never seen such false sincerity. He wanted to do something but couldn't. This was just kids playing a friendly game . . . wasn't it?

"Maybe you should wear a bucket up top next time, like the rest of your lamebrain friends," Tommy added, and his buddies burst out laughing again.

Swift and Lucas were first to reach Gordon. He was dazed, struggling to get up. Each grabbed under his arms and helped him. Lucas wondered how it was that Gordon wasn't crying after that.

But he wasn't crying—he was smiling.

Gordon stood up and brushed off his sweater—the one that looked like it had been handed down through a dozen hockey players. The "9" on the back had been ripped again, and the top was now even more unstitched and sagging.

"I wasn't sure about that number 9 anyway," Gordon said, giving Swift a big grin and a wink, which surprised both Lucas and Edna. "Picking a number is like picking which way you shoot—takes some time." Lucas had noticed that, too. Gordon had just started skating, but already he shot both ways—sometimes left, sometimes right. Hardly any of the pros could even do that! "Let's play?" Gordon asked, smiling. He was ready to jump back in the game.

Back in position, he dusted the snow off his pants and leaned on his stick, pausing only to look up, once and hard, toward Tommy, who was back by his own net, laughing at something he had said to the goaltender.

Back and forth the play went, with each out player taking a turn carrying the puck and trying to set up a goal. The two teams were now tied 4–4. Next goal would win.

Tommy had the puck behind his own net. He was coming up the ice hard, stickhandling easily. And he was skating straight at Lucas. Just as Lucas was going to try a poke check, Tommy niftily slipped the puck between Lucas's skates and was past him in a heartbeat.

And then he wasn't.

It was as if Tommy had deliberately skated into a brick wall. From out of nowhere, Gordon appeared directly in his path. Gordon did nothing. He just let Tommy crash into him.

It all seemed to take place in slow motion. Tommy's face went into Gordon's chest, and then, just as happens in cartoons, Tommy seemed to melt and slide off the immovable Gordon like snow off a roof.

He slid to the ice and began whimpering.

"Sorry," Gordon said to him as he lay there. "Accident."

Gordon picked up the puck, skated down ice with it, and with his long reach, used one hand on the stick to sweep it around the other goaltender and in past the rubber boots.

It was 5–4 for Gordon, Edna, and the Ice Chips.

Gordon skated calmly back to his sister, a big smile on his face.

"Let's go home," he said.

CHAPTER 14

"That kid's gonna be great," Lucas said as the three Chips watched Gordon and Edna head off across the field—Gordon with his "new" skates once again slung over his neck.

"That hockey sweater he had on under his coat was really ratty. The number was even peeling off," said Edge. He wasn't trying to be critical. He just felt bad for the guy.

"Didn't matter, though, did it?" said Lucas. *Maybe equipment doesn't matter as much as I'd thought.*

The wind was picking up again, snow once more starting to fall. Lucas turned to Swift and noticed a wet drop falling from her left eye. She must have had a snowflake blow into her eye. Or was that a tear?

"Let's go for one more skate," she said.

"Shouldn't we try the comm-bands again?" asked Edge, who'd had to give Gordon back his coat. He was still warm from the game and the skating, but soon he'd be shivering again. "We should try to reach Crunch—reach *someone*."

"In a minute?" said Swift, making sure she'd properly adjusted her goalie pads after Edna had worn them. "Can we just skate for a minute?"

"Yes!" Edge and Lucas agreed at exactly the same moment.

Tommy and his gang were still gathering up their equipment and trudging slowly up the embankment. Lucas couldn't help thinking that Tommy had shrunk since he'd run into that brick wall called Gordon.

There was something else, too. It seemed that the other kids with Tommy weren't sticking as close to him as before. Two had already run ahead. The third was shaking his head as he walked off in another direction.

Maybe, just maybe, Tommy's days as the town bully were done.

Lucas pushed off, and the wind, funnelling down the field and along the frozen slough, caught under his arms and half-lifted, half-hurled him down the ice. He put his skates together, both pointing straight ahead, and just let the wind take him.

I'm sailing! Lucas thought. *Sailing on skates.*

He could hear Swift shrieking with delight as the wind caught her, too. Lucas looked back. Both Swift and Edge were following his example of just putting their skates together and letting it happen.

Swift reached out to Edge and took his hand. She put an arm around him to keep him warm. They pumped a

few times to catch up to Lucas, and Swift took Lucas's hand with her free one.

Laughing, shrieking, shouting, the three Chips sailed down the slough and smashed into the soft snowdrift that had built up at the far end. All three were buried completely in the snow and came up shaking it free and laughing hysterically.

Now, thought Lucas, *that is something you can't do in an indoor rink*. No wonder Bompa got so excited whenever he showed Lucas those grainy old photographs of kids holding hands and drift-skating on an iced-over lake.

The photographs, with everyone frozen still, hadn't been able to convey what it felt like. But now Lucas knew for himself. He knew what Bompa had meant. He'd have to tell him that now he understood.

Then it struck him. *How will I tell Bompa? How are we going to get home?*

"Let's go again!" Swift shouted, shaking the snow out of her ponytail.

The three began skating back toward the other end. Only now, they were going against the wind. It was hard work and getting harder, with the wind picking up. Edge put his hands in his armpits again and hunched his shoulders.

The wind blew even stronger, and the three put their heads down and dug in as hard as they could. Swift dropped Lucas's hand and pushed off, eyes closed with the effort.

And then, in an instant, they found themselves crossing the centre line in the old Riverton arena.

They tried to stop as best they could, but they were going fast—too fast, now that they were no longer fighting the wind. Edge and Swift smacked into each other and fell to the ground. And Lucas kept going . . . straight into the boards.

CHAPTER 15
Riverton

"That's *unbelievable*! I don't believe any of it!"

Crunch was laughing so hard he had a cramp in his side. His tablet bounced with him as he giggled, and the images it was recording were shaking, too.

"That's completely, utterly *bananas*!" he said, sliding his glasses up into his thick black hair so he could wipe the tears from his eyes.

"It's true!" protested Lucas. He also seemed close to tears, but for a different reason.

"How gullible do you think I am?" asked Crunch. "I watched you skate over the red line, all the way to the boards. *I recorded it.* How can you expect me to believe you flew off in a *time machine* and played some game on a frozen pond?"

"Slough," Swift corrected.

"*Slough*?" Crunch said, shaking his head. "Is that even a real word, or is it one of Edge's made-up ones?"

"Oh, just forget it, then!" said an exasperated Edge. "We don't care if you believe us. It's true and we know it's true."

But is it? Lucas wondered. It sure didn't seem to make sense now. But how could three people have exactly the same dream at the same time? And in the middle of a skating race? *Impossible!*

"I've got it all here, don't forget!" said Crunch, tapping the side of his tablet. He'd already stopped the recording and was calling it up on the screen. Edge slid over on the bench toward Crunch while Lucas and Swift gathered around him. "I'll *show* you," Crunch said confidently.

The camera was focused on the rink—first the right side, then the left, where Swift, Edge, and Lucas had just stopped. Swift pushes away, suggests they race . . . and they all take off. They pass the blue line and then hit the red centre line—all three of them at once. There's a slight flicker, as if the video has skipped a frame. And then there they are, across the line, falling all over each other and slamming into the boards.

"Awesome crash, Top Shelf," Edge said, smiling at the video.

Edge was too busy falling when Lucas, with barely enough time to turn his shoulder, had crashed almost face-first into the boards. Edge had tried to stop on his own when he'd reappeared, but that's when Swift had plowed right into him from behind. Together, they'd spun around, their arms reaching to grab hold of something, and had both fallen flat on their bums.

"Did you edit it?" Swift asked suspiciously, squinting at the screen. Maybe it was *Crunch's* story they should be questioning.

Crunch set his tablet down and stared at her. "Do you think I had time to do that?" he asked, confused.

Lucas knew that if he were the Ice Chip who'd stayed behind, he wouldn't believe the story either. It simply made no sense.

Why didn't we bring anything back with us as proof?

That's when Lucas remembered his quarter—the one that was now from 1936. The proof *was* there—in his pocket!

He pulled his gloves off and threw them down on the stands in front of him. He reached into his pocket just as the main doors of the rink burst open with a loud clack.

Quiet Dave the Iceman was back . . . and he had Sadie with him.

* * *

"You kids are NOT allowed in *here!*" the Iceman yelled. Halfway through the sentence, his voice had cracked, as if he wasn't used to yelling at people and didn't know how.

Lucas hunched over immediately, a guilty look on his face. Edge just stared back in disbelief.

They'd been caught.

And they were about to be in big, big trouble.

Dave had Sadie by the elbow—he must have found her on his way back into the arena. In his other hand was an enormous white towel, the kind someone might put on the back of a flooding machine before it cleaned a rink. That's what Dave must have gone home to get. He'd been faster than expected, and now he was back—and Scratch had . . . they'd gone and . . . how would they explain what they'd done?

Did Dave already know?

Sadie looked at Swift. She had fear in her eyes. She was trembling. Had she been crying? Slowly, Sadie shook her head in Swift's direction.

"She didn't tell him anything," Swift whispered to the others, translating her sister's gestures. "He doesn't know that we have my dad's keys."

They should have given Sadie a comm-band when she left—at least to make sure she'd arrived home safely, Lucas thought, kicking himself.

Where has Sadie been all this time? he wondered, worried. And then he remembered: they were the only ones who had experienced the time in Saskatoon with Edna and Gordon. As far as Crunch was concerned, Sadie had left only ten minutes ago.

It could take that long just to walk around the building.

Dave had probably caught Sadie near the Zamboni exit.

And he must have missed Lars, Lucas realized, relieved. Lars hadn't seen the rink—all beautiful and perfect—and Lucas didn't want him to see it. He didn't want to share any of this moment with Lars—this perfect moment that he now felt he'd stolen.

They'd stolen it, and Dave had caught them.

Suddenly, Sadie freed herself from Dave's grip and threw herself toward the Plexiglas by the far gate in the boards. Her face was twisted . . . into a smile? *What?* She wasn't crying now—she was banging on the glass, beaming.

"*Whooooo did this?*" Sadie yelled toward the Ice Chips, grinning at the now perfect ice. "HOW?" she yelled back at Dave, who didn't seem to have noticed she'd escaped.

That's because Dave, too, was staring at the rink. Only he wasn't surprised like Sadie.

He looked very, very worried.

CHAPTER 16

"Guys, the ice!" Swift yelled. Then she jumped back through the hole in the boards as fast as she could. What else could she do? Dave had already found them out, but he couldn't drag them home to their parents if he couldn't catch them on the ice.

Or . . . in Saskatoon!

Edge couldn't believe she'd take the risk.

"Swift! *What* are you doing?!" He glared after her and then turned back toward Lucas for support.

But Lucas wasn't watching Swift. He wasn't watching Sadie, either, as she bent down on the other side of the rink, opened her skate bag, and rushed to lace up her skates—the freshly flooded ice too delicious to ignore. No, Lucas was watching Dave, who was now angrily marching toward them.

"He's going to tell our parents," moaned Crunch, running his fingers through his hair in a panic, forgetting that he'd left his glasses on top of his head. "They're going to find out, and I'm going to be grounded."

"Just *wait* . . ." Lucas said quietly to Crunch and Edge, slowly raising his hand out to his side like a crossing guard.

Maybe we aren't in trouble—at least, not the usual kind.

Lucas didn't know why he had that feeling. He just did.

Edge, however, couldn't wait. Not knowing who to protect—Lucas and Crunch from Dave, or Swift and Sadie from another leap through time—he bounded back onto the ice, ready for whatever happened next.

Soon Dave was in front of the stands, in front of Lucas and Crunch, looking unbelievably stressed.

"What you've done is dangerous—*incredibly* DANGER-OUS! Do you understand that?!" Dave said loudly. He was dragging his big white towel with him like a blankie.

"I *guess* . . . I mean, yes," Lucas answered. In his skates, he was almost the height of Dave's shoulders, but that didn't make him feel any better. Lying and getting caught always made Lucas feel as small as a mouse. Embarrassed, he kept his eyes on Dave's towel so he wouldn't have to look the Iceman in the eyes.

Wait! Dave knows we cleaned the rink, but does he already know what Scratch can do? Where he can go? He must!

Lucas was putting the pieces together as fast as he could. He paused for a moment . . . and then went for it.

"We . . . we found Scratch around the corner—Crunch did," Lucas suddenly confessed.

"*Lucas!*" moaned Crunch, cupping his forehead in the palms of his hands. "I'm not the one who—"

"Then we used our hockey towels, put them on the back," Lucas continued, ignoring Crunch. "We fixed Scratch . . . and then he . . . cleaned the *ice*." Lucas let this last word fall out of his mouth like a drop of water from a dripping tap—a dull thud with a question mark. There was more to this story and he knew it.

Dave looked like he might yell again, but he didn't. He turned around and rubbed his hand over his chin, and when he turned back, he was Dave the Iceman again. Defeated, he offered Lucas a frustrated smile—as though to say, "What's done is done."

"Look, kids, this rink is . . . *broken*," he said carefully. "It's *closed*. This is the end."

Was that relief Lucas sensed? Or sadness? He couldn't tell.

"It doesn't have to be the end," Lucas offered, trying to be optimistic. He desperately wanted to talk about the time machine, but he didn't know how.

"I'm afraid it does, Lucas," said Dave. "I found some old-style fuses at that Whatsit Shop in town, but now I can't even get into the chiller room because the city—*the mayor*—took away my key for that door. So what you've seen here tonight . . . that was this rink's last flood."

"Or . . . not!"

It was Crunch, suddenly standing at Lucas's side with his tablet under his arm. He was excited, as if he'd just solved a hard math problem or discovered a new planet.

"The chiller room is behind that big blue steel door, right? The one you hit with the puck, Lucas?"

Lucas and Dave both nodded.

"Well, in that case"—Crunch grinned and cleared his throat—"I think we might be able to help you."

* * *

"Don't get mad," Crunch warned, looking at Dave. Then he turned to Lucas. "I noticed this when I was still looking for the broom, after the shootout."

Carefully, Crunch reached his hand out toward the blue metal door and turned the doorknob slightly. It twisted, detached, and then fell to the ground with a metallic thud.

Lucas's cheeks flushed red. The knob must have come loose after he'd slammed it with the puck!

Crunch looked over, and Lucas nodded and moved toward him. Together, the two boys gave the metal door a heavy check with their shoulders. Something clicked where the door handle used to be—and the door gave.

Slowly, it began to open.

Good, thought Lucas. *Swift can keep her keys hidden.*

Dave might not tell anyone that they'd broken into the rink, but he'd definitely have to tell Swift's dad that his keys had been stolen.

Dave looked upset about the door, but he seemed to realize that he couldn't react that way because the Chips were helping him. Instead, he put his hand into his pocket and pulled out several small glass bottles of slightly different sizes and shapes.

"These are the fuses," Dave said, jostling them around a little in the palm of his hand. "They're safety devices. If a surge of electricity is too strong, the fuses burn out and need replacing. The Whatsit Shop's got boxes of them—all different kinds. I haven't changed a chiller fuse in ages and couldn't remember the size, so your mother just gave me a handful."

Lucas had to stifle a laugh. *Bits and bobs for the oddest jobs*, he repeated in his head. He was sure that his parents had *no* idea how odd this job was.

As Dave sifted through the fuses, he told them that he hadn't even had a chance to see if any of them fit before his key had been taken and the rink closed. "I think it's either one of these round ones or the one with the yellow—" he started.

"That one," said Crunch with complete certainty, poking his finger down into Dave's palm and touching one of the small glass objects. Then to Lucas: "What did you think I was looking up on my tablet?"

"Thanks," said Dave. "But this is just the first step. Even if this fuse works, I'll still need to find a belt for the pump—one that fits."

But the Chips already knew the answer to that: *No one had been able to find one anywhere.*

* * *

With her arms out to her sides, Sadie skated over to the goal line, where Edge and her sister were standing, and wrapped her arms around Swift. They hugged each other as they turned once together on the ice.

"Are you . . . okay?" Edge could hear Swift whisper into her sister's white fluffy sweater before they separated.

Sadie nodded to say that she was. In fact, now she was ecstatic—she couldn't believe what she was skating on!

Edge and Swift watched, mesmerized, as Sadie's blades glided across the crisp surface of the rink, her legs criss-crossing in a fluid motion as she flipped from backwards skating to forwards nearing the centre ice line.

She was getting ready to jump . . .

"*Sadie, nooo!*" Edge suddenly called out, remembering where they were—what could happen on this ice.

But it was too late.

Sadie put all her weight on her right leg, swung her left one around to turn halfway, and then dug the toe pick of her left skate hard into the ice. As she vaulted her body into the air, she crossed the centre line in mid-flight . . .

. . . and landed cleanly on the other side.

Swift and Edge turned to each other. Their hearts were beating so fast, they were almost in their throats.

How had Sadie crossed the line without—? Wait! Had they missed seeing the flicker?

"Do you think she jumped *here* and then jumped again in Saskatoon, at *exactly* the right time?" asked Edge, looking at Swift as he went over each thought. "*Simultenaciously*? Or something like that?"

"Impossible," Swift said. Then she called out to Sadie: "How's the . . . ice?" There was suspicion in Swift's voice—and worry—but she had to know.

"AH-mazing!" Sadie replied enthusiastically as she circled again, her speed blowing her curly brown hair across her face. Completely oblivious to the fact that something magical had happened on that very spot only moments earlier, Sadie turned twice more and did another toe loop over the centre line.

In the corner of the arena, Dave looked sheepishly at Lucas, as if he wanted to say something but thought he shouldn't.

"Wait, did she just—?" Lucas started, but he, too, was afraid to continue.

Crunch, on the other hand, hadn't even noticed that Sadie had crossed the centre line. All he'd seen, spinning through the air, was Sadie's outfit—specifically, her figure skating tights.

What did Lucas say about Little Robert and the invention with the belt? Crunch still didn't believe that his teammates had found a time machine, but Lucas's story had given him an idea.

Crunch was about to call out to Sadie—to see if she had another pair of nylons or tights in her skate bag—when Dave suddenly blurted: "Don't worry, Lucas. She's fine. It only works right after the flood . . . That's when you travel through time."

"Through what?!" Crunch said, nearly choking.

CHAPTER 17

Butterflies in the stomach . . .

Lucas wondered where on earth that saying had come from. His mother had asked him if he had "butterflies in his tummy" before he headed off to the Riverton Community Arena for the fall tryouts.

No, he didn't have *butterflies* in his tummy. He had crocodiles and pterodactyls and *Tyrannosaurus rexes* and wildcats and boa constrictors and at least one angry ape with a big ugly sliver in his bum cheek!

But that was good, Lucas thought. You *should* be nervous. Nerves make you sharp. They make you go harder, try harder, play better. Nerves make you want it—whatever *it* was—all the more.

Lucas knew what he was aiming for: a place on the Ice Chips.

He definitely didn't want to play for the Riverton Stars. He didn't want to play with the Blitz twins, or with Lars—Lars was the worst. "I'd better make the Ice Chips,"

Lucas chanted as he rubbed his lucky quarter (the quarter that was back to saying 2002 . . . *he had no idea how!*).

Lars and the Blitz twins can have the Stars.

To make the Ice Chips this season, Lucas knew he'd have to make a real impression. There was no other option—even while his face still burned like he'd fallen asleep on a beach without sunscreen on. It was windburn from when the wind had whipped them down that frozen slough—Swift and Edge had it, too.

Lucas couldn't believe how much had happened since then.

Dave had fixed the chillers in the Riverton Community Arena with the fuse, and then he'd fixed the pumps using Sadie's figure skating nylons as a belt for the motor. Lucas was surprised that it had all worked, but it had. And the Ice Chips had helped! Soon, the machines were freezing again, and Mayor Ward had reopened their arena.

But not just that: it was *their rink* where this morning's novice tryouts were being held.

Their rink. Their ice. And Lucas and Edge on the same line again—or so they hoped.

As Lucas packed Speedy's stinking, mismatched equipment into his bag, he knew he'd never been so ready to compete.

* * *

There was motion everywhere at the Riverton Community Arena—players moving toward the dressing rooms, parents moving toward the stands, and the rink's regular Zamboni (*not Scratch—thank goodness!*) making slick, glossy half ovals around the ice.

Lucas knew the flood wouldn't be as beautiful as Scratch's, but it would be good enough. And his freshly sharpened skates would help.

Lucas's parents and Connor took their seats in the stands as he made his way down the hall toward the dressing room.

Swift was probably already there, tightening her purple laces beside an empty spot on the bench—the spot she always saved for Lucas.

And Edge had almost certainly arrived early, as he always did. He'd be dressed and sitting in the stands, quietly thinking about the game, just as his father used to do before his field hockey games. Mr. Singh had a name for it, but Lucas couldn't quite remember it. "Envisioning"? Or "imaging"? He almost had it, but it didn't matter. That was Edge's tradition, not his.

Lucas had his own routine to think about: he had to touch the old photograph of the championship team in the trophy case, wipe his hand over the ledge of the skate sharpener's shop, and straighten that crooked picture frame for luck. His pre-game ritual.

This wasn't exactly a game, but Lucas knew he'd need all the luck he could get.

* * *

All through the arena, the kids were preparing for tryouts.

When the doors to the rink opened, the kids flooded into it with cheers.

On the ice, players from both leagues swirled around Lucas, greeting each other, talking about what they'd done over the summer, and boasting about the new equipment they'd bought.

The old pants Lucas was wearing were black rather than the light blue the Ice Chips normally wore, and one of his shin pads was still cracked, but for some reason, he didn't care.

He was just glad to be there, to be soaking it in.

Crunch and Swift skated up to Lucas, and all three pounded gloves. Soon, Edge was there, too, moving back and forth on his skates—eager to get going.

* * *

Fweee-uuurllll!

A whistle blew at centre ice.

Lucas swallowed hard, pushing those raging pterodactyls back down where they belonged. He took a deep breath and skated with the other kids to surround the coach in charge of the tryouts. The kids looked like bees hurrying to the honey hive.

"Okay, boys and girls," the on-ice coach said. "You know the drills. We're going to divide you into groups and see how you do. No need to be nervous. Just enjoy yourselves—and good luck!"

No need to be nervous, Lucas thought. *Ha!*

Up in the stands, the coaches and assistant coaches, the team managers, and the executive of the minor hockey system were all holding clipboards on their laps and staring down at the ice. On each clipboard was a sheet of paper listing the names of all the players, along with the numbers they'd been assigned in the dressing rooms. There were boxes in which the judges could mark the players on skating, shooting, stickhandling, passing, and other skills.

Both Mr. Blitz and Coach Small were up there with them.

Still nervous, Lucas looked around at the other players in his group, sizing them up, trying to see where he fit in.

There was Alex Stepanov—"Dynamo"—the tiny forward from Moscow, Russia, who was still learning English when he'd joined the Ice Chips two years ago. He was good—no, great—but small.

And Maurice "Slapper" Boudreau. He had a great slapshot and was huge. Just *huge*. He played defence for the Chips and was already as big as some ten-year-olds, but he was a slow skater.

Edge was there, too.

And then there were some new kids from school:

Dylan Chung—*had he really come out?*—and Tianna Foster. Tianna, who was born in Jamaica but had just moved to Riverton from Chicago, seemed to be able to skate, but she was holding her stick all wrong. And Dylan, the non-stop talker, looked like he might have a great wrist shot if he could focus on the puck long enough.

There was another girl, too, but Lucas hadn't caught her name because Dylan was talking. And now her face was turned away from him . . .

Wait—*Sadie?!*

"You seriously think I'd give up this ice . . . *after that night?*" Sadie whispered with a smile, giving Lucas a friendly punch in the shoulder. Figure skating, she said, was still going to be held at Mr. Blitz's synthetic rink—the fake ice she already knew she hated—so she'd simply decided to switch sports.

"You can call me 'Blades,'" she said, grinning, just as the coach announced the final member of their group . . .

Lars Larsson.

Lucas had actually shivered.

CHAPTER 18

Fweee-uuurllll!

The coach's whistle blew again, and the skills tests began.

First was to skate around the faceoff circles, where pylons had been placed a few feet apart. The players were to weave around the pylons and try to do it fast. Edge was fastest, but Lucas wasn't far behind. Nor was Sadie.

Lucas secretly wished that Lars—*horrible Lars*—would fall and then quit in a huff like he had at their "final skate," but he didn't. Lars, too, was at Lucas's heels.

The players then moved to the next station, where they had to stickhandle a puck toward a hockey stick that was lying on two small stacks of pucks—one stack at each end, like posts. The players were to let their pucks slide under the stick while they hopped over it. Then they'd scoop their pucks up again on the other side.

Lucas fell on his first attempt, got up, and noticed the Blitz twins, Jared and Beatrice, smirking at him. Luckily,

Lars had been busy looking into the stands at a blonde woman who, if her face was any sign, had a few pterodactyls of her own. *That must be his mother*, Lucas thought as he brushed himself off.

"You okay?" a voice called out—it was Tianna. "I'm sure you'll get it next try."

"Thanks," said Lucas. He was embarrassed but ready to go again.

Tianna offered him a warm smile. "I've only ever played roller derby. I can skate, but I'm not doing too well with the stick. Any tips?"

"I guess . . . don't worry about what anyone else thinks." That was all Lucas could come up with.

Then they were on to the next round.

Lucas was terrific on the third drill, where they stick-handled around the pylons. He'd always had good hands, and it seemed that this year he was even better. Edge was great and handled the drill effortlessly. Dylan was surprisingly good, and Tianna fumbled her way through—Sadie, too.

And then it was Lars's turn. He lost the puck several times and knocked over three pylons!

Lucas didn't think that should make him happy, but it did.

Was he turning into a bully, too?

* * *

Up next were the faceoffs.

In a far corner of the rink, one of the helpers was having players from two groups face off against each other. Edge was called to face off against Beatrice Blitz and—just as Lucas knew he would—used his old trick of plucking the puck out of mid-air just before it bounced on the ice.

Edge moved so fast he was like a cat reaching out from under a sofa to swat a dangled string.

Lucas couldn't help laughing, but no sooner had the laugh popped out of his throat than he felt something burning into his cheeks.

It was the stare of Beatrice Blitz—angry, furious, wicked, nasty, ugly, and *mean*.

"Lucas," the coach helper called out, checking his list of players. "And Lars."

Lucas's heart sank like a stone.

He skated over to the faceoff spot, his cheeks still burning from Beatrice's nasty stare. Lars was skating in from the other side.

Lucas was certain that Lars had briefly turned to look over at his mother.

The two young players faced each other. The assistant held the puck out for what seemed like forever—long enough for Lucas to glance up and see that Lars was more scared than he was.

The puck dropped, seemingly in slow motion, like a round black balloon coming down from the ceiling. Lars

reacted too quickly, probably trying to cuff it out of the air as Edge had done, but in moving too fast he had just cuffed air. His stick was well off the ice when the puck slapped down flat and *stayed*—perfectly—on Lucas's stick blade. Lucas stickhandled twice, then tried a little puck flip back onto the blade—and for once, it worked. He held out his blade with the puck and the helper took it, his eyes open wide.

"You're *good*!" the young helper said.

Lucas felt his cheeks burn again—but this time, it felt great.

Frowning, Lars just turned and skated away.

The next to face off were Crunch and Dynamo. Lucas wanted to go and talk to Edge about his nifty little move and began skating over toward his friends.

But then down he went!

He hit the ice hard, his helmet bouncing off the solid surface and his shoulder stinging. He then slid into the boards right beside Edge, turning quickly to see what on earth he had stepped on.

Lars was bending down to retrieve his stick. He was grinning. Right behind him, Beatrice Blitz was sticking out her tongue.

"Sorry," Lars said. "It was an accident."

Who does Lars think he is? Tommy Boland from Saskatoon?

Lucas struggled to his feet as Lars and Beatrice skated away.

"That was *no* accident," Edge said. "He meant to trip you. And I'll bet that sneaky little Beatrice put him up to it."

Lucas turned to stare after his "tripper." Beatrice was off with her brother, Jared, obviously telling him what a great thing Lars had just done to that "loser" Lucas. But Lars wasn't with them.

He was over near his mother and she was ripping into him. She looked angry—maybe even embarrassed—but she was keeping her voice down so Lucas couldn't hear what she was saying.

Next thing Lucas knew, Lars was skating back toward him and Edge—and this time, *his* cheeks were the ones that were burning. He looked like he was about to cry.

Lars skated up, stopped, and stuttered, "I'm . . . really . . . *sorry*." He almost spat out the last word—the one that counted.

Is he sorry?

Then he skated away quickly, his cheeks flaming.

Edge looked at Lucas, his eyes as wide as pucks.

"What was *that*?" Lucas said, stunned.

❖ ❖ ❖

The fate of each player now rested on a dozen or more clipboards. The tryouts were over and done with, and there was nothing anyone could do but wait to see which team he or she'd been placed on.

Lucas was confident that Swift and Edge would be on the Ice Chips again. Swift was perfect in goal during the shootout—the last drill—and Edge had impressed the coaches as usual. Lucas didn't think he'd made any serious mistakes, apart from that one little stumble over that stick lying on the stacks of pucks, but he couldn't be sure.

And then there was Lars . . .

Lars had done some things well—really, *really* well. But he'd also had some problems. Lucas couldn't tell what the coaches had thought of him.

"Don't worry . . . Lars will be perfect for the Stars," Swift said quietly, grinning as she patted Lucas's helmet and they followed the other players into the dressing room.

CHAPTER 19

BZZZZZZZZZZZZZ!

Lucas had just finished packing his shoulder pads and skates into his bag when his comm-band buzzed.

Then it buzzed again.

And then Swift's. And then Crunch's.

"Ugh, what is he doing?" Lucas asked as he let go of his hockey bag zipper and raised his wrist to answer his comm.

Lucas, Swift, and Crunch were still in the dressing room, laughing over the drills and enjoying themselves, but Edge—who undressed faster than anyone else on the team—had gone off into the public part of the arena to find his parents. And now he wouldn't stop buzzing!

"What?!" Lucas half-shouted into his comm-band, laughing. He knew the lists of who'd made which team hadn't been posted yet—that's all the other players were talking about. Why couldn't Edge just follow the coaches' instructions like everyone else: try to relax and hang out while he waited for the results?

"This isn't about the teams," Edge said, breathless, whispering. "Come out here—*now*. There's something you've got to see."

* * *

Edge had asked them to meet at the skate sharpener's— *immediately!* So Swift, Crunch, and Lucas had all rushed over. But then there they were, just standing and wait- ing: watching Quiet Dave drill a new hole in the freshly painted wall outside the closed shop.

What was the rush?

Unless . . .

Lucas hadn't wanted to tell his friends that he was worried about his ritual all through tryouts. Before he'd stepped onto the ice, he'd touched the trophy case and run his hand along the ledge at the skate sharpener's, just as he'd planned. But the frame he usually straightened had been missing—was still missing. Lucas guessed it had been taken down to repaint the arena, now that their rink was open again, but what had that meant for his luck today?

"You're never going to believe this," Edge said as he snuck up behind them, smiling. "Lucas, this is going to blow your mind."

When Dave's hole was drilled, a few inches higher than before, he put in a screw and bent down to pick up the picture frame—the one Lucas always straightened.

Dave held out the frame with both arms . . . and turned it around.

That's when Lucas's mouth dropped open.

His hands started sweating. And the hairs on the back of his neck stood up.

Edge was right!

What was inside the frame was no longer a black-and-white photograph of old skates. Now there was a faded pencil drawing with lines, shapes, and arrows—*a blueprint*. The page looked like it had been folded many times, and its corners were worn. It was *old* . . .

But it wasn't! Was it?

"That's—" Lucas sputtered as Dave placed the frame on the screw and turned around to face the Ice Chips.

Lucas couldn't believe it. It was the drawing that little kid had pulled from his back pocket in that dimly lit garage in Saskatoon. It was a picture of the skate-sharpening machine that Robert and Mr. Ward had been building . . . *in 1936!*

"But that belongs to—" Lucas said, staring at the drawing and barely moving. He was confused—really confused.

"It *belonged* to my father," Dave said with an awkward smile.

* * *

On the night of the final skate, Lucas had eventually told Dave *everything*—everything he could remember.

He'd told Dave about Saskatoon, about Gordon and Edna's second-hand skates, about the trip to the skate sharpener's house, about Little Robert, about his quarter, and even about the bully, Tommy Boland.

At the mention of Gordon's and Edna's names, Dave's face had flushed red, but Lucas didn't know why.

"Gordon? Are you sure?" Dave asked in his quietest voice.

"Yes, Gordon," Lucas repeated.

What is Dave so worried about? Lucas wondered. *The Ice Chips are all safe . . . all back home.*

But before the Chips left the rink that night, Dave had made Lucas promise never to time-travel again. Then he'd made him promise to make Edge and Swift promise. And Crunch, too. They would never use Scratch, touch Scratch, even *look* at Scratch again—and they would never tell anyone what they'd done or where they'd gone.

Lucas had nodded, but he hadn't said anything out loud.

"Edge asked me about the frame—he called it *your* frame—during tryouts. And that gave me an idea," Dave said now. "After hearing about Saskatoon . . . well, I thought *this* picture might have a little more meaning for you."

"*Fan-tabulous*," Edge said, watching to see Lucas's reaction.

"Robert—*Little Robert*, as you called him—grew up and had a son," Dave continued, amused. "That was me."

"Is he serious?" Crunch said, turning to Swift. He still had trouble believing that Lucas and the others had travelled through time. And Dave's story was even more bananas.

Lucas watched as Edge reached out and unstraightened the blueprint—to make sure it was crooked. Then he nodded in Lucas's direction.

"Go, Lucas! Do your thing!" Swift said eagerly, giving him a gentle push. "The lists are almost up!"

Lucas stepped forward, his mind reeling. The sign outside the sharpener's shop in Saskatoon had said "Ward's Sharpening." And Dave the Iceman was Dave Ward. *They were related!*

"Lucas!" Swift said hurriedly.

Lucas reached up and carefully tilted his lucky frame to the right, then a little to the left . . . until it was perfectly straight. The ritual.

But am I too late?

Dave didn't seem to think so.

"You know, those kids you met out on the frozen slough?" he continued happily, keeping his voice down. "Well, they grew up, too."

"Edna and Gordon?" Edge asked, excited. He couldn't wait to hear.

Dave lowered his voice even further. "Yes, the brother and sister: Edna and Gordie Howe."

Edge nearly fell over backwards. Swift shook her head in shock. And Lucas . . . Lucas had tears in his eyes.

"Gordie—who?" asked Crunch, blinking, wondering if he'd misheard.

Dave's childlike smile appeared as he spoke: "Gordon didn't just grow up to become a hockey player. He grew up to become the best hockey player in the world."

GORDIE HOWE

CHAPTER 20

"The lists are *up!*"

Sadie screeched excitedly as she pushed her way into the middle of their group and nearly leaped into her sister's arms. "I'm on your team!! *I'm on your team!!*"

"You made it?!" said Swift with a huge grin on her face.

Edge and Crunch both cheered and gave Sadie high-fives, but it took Lucas a second to realize what was happening—that this was the moment he'd been waiting for, that the big answer had arrived.

Stars . . . or Ice Chips.

Or neither. That could happen, too.

Lucas had been so busy thinking about Gordon that he'd almost forgotten why they were at the arena in the first place. Dave's story was too amazing: big, goofy Gordon, who'd just been learning to stand on those over-sized skates in Saskatoon, was really Gordie Howe!

Now *that* was magical!

Lucas's dad often read him stories about great hockey players—sometimes from books, sometimes just from the backs of hockey cards. And Gordie Howe, "Number 9," was one of the greatest! He was called "Mr. Hockey," and he'd won four Stanley Cups—*four!* He'd set tons of records and he'd played more than a *thousand* NHL games. Even Wayne Gretzky had admired him!

Lucas had looked up to him, too—even when Gordon had had just one skate, out on the slough!

* * *

But the *lists* . . .

Lucas swallowed hard—the pterodactyls were back and they were going nuts!

If only his luck would help him out . . .

Sadie said she wouldn't tell them—she didn't want to spoil the surprise. They'd have to look for themselves.

Lucas looked at Swift. They did a fist tap for luck, and then all four Ice Chips—they *hoped* they were still Ice Chips—joined the other anxious kids flooding into the hallway to get a look at the arena's bulletin board.

Lucas went at it backwards. First he scanned the list for Mr. Blitz's Riverton Stars. No "Lucas." Deep breath. Beat back the pterodactyls.

Then he came to the list that meant everything: the Riverton Ice Chips, coached by George Small.

Swift's name was at the very top as the goaltender of the Ice Chips. And Edge was there, right below her.

And . . . Lucas!

The crocodiles and pterodactyls—and that very angry ape with the sliver in his butt cheek—vanished instantly.

But then they roared back . . .

Halfway down the list was a name neither Swift nor Lucas nor Edge had ever for a moment expected to see—one they wished they hadn't seen.

Lars.

* * *

"Dylan and Tianna made the Ice Chips, too," said Edge, trying to cheer up Lucas. "That means lots of new players, not just—"

"The bully," said Lucas, looking worried.

Most of the players who were now leaving the arena were pounding fists and congratulating each other—talking, shouting, cheering. Others seemed disappointed. One or two looked like they might cry when they got home.

Lucas needed a distraction. That much was obvious to Swift, Edge, and Crunch (the Chips' science genius had made the team too!).

"Hey, Lucas, on the night of our last skate, where do you think Dave the Iceman was going?" Edge said quickly, as though the thought had only just occurred to him.

"Home to get that towel?" Lucas answered.

"No, I mean . . . he was going to flood the rink for himself, wasn't he? To go *where*? And do *what*?" Edge loved a good mystery, and he knew Lucas did, too.

Lucas just shrugged his shoulders. He didn't know. All he was thinking was: *Lars is going to be an Ice Chip!*

"If this bonkers time-travel story is true," said Crunch, sounding doubtful, but also like he was enjoying Edge's game, "then who do you think Quiet Dave's met already? Bobby Orr? Wayne Gretzky? Mario Lemieux? Who?"

"Who would *you* want to meet?" Swift said to Crunch. Then, turning to Edge and Lucas with a quizzical smile, she asked, "And if you could leap again, *would* you?"

Edge raised one of his eyebrows and smiled. *Yeah, of course I would.*

Lucas was about to say that Dave had made him promise not to, but he paused when he saw that Swift had extended her arm toward him.

In the palm of her hand—shining, almost winking at him—were Mr. Bertrand's rink keys.

ACKNOWLEDGEMENTS

Thank you to Suzanne Sutherland for her careful guidance in editing and shaping our journey from Riverton's magical ice rink to a slough in Saskatchewan; to Maeve O'Regan in publicity; and to Jennifer Lambert for her support. And thanks to the rest of the wonderful team at HarperCollins, who made this time travel possible: Janice Weaver, our keen-eyed copyeditor; Stephanie Nuñez, our patient and well-organized production editor; and Lloyd Davis, our proofreader. Thank you also to Bruce Westwood and Meg Wheeler at Westwood Creative Artists for their guidance and friendship.

Thanks to the many friends and new acquaintances who lent us their stories so we could shape the characters on the Ice Chips team: Manmeet Singh, who grew up with Kerry; Jagdeep Mann and his son, Himmit, for their stories and photos; and Harnarayan Singh, the host of *Hockey Night in Canada: Punjabi Edition*, who helped us get in touch with some young Sikh hockey families, including

Gurinder Singh Marwaha and his son, Jeevan, and Rumnik Chana and her sons, Hazoor and Nihal.

Thank you also to Kim Smith, whose beautiful illustrations were possibly the most magical part for us.

And thank you to our families, who made it possible for us to keep our heads in the snow clouds all year long.

—Roy MacGregor and Kerry MacGregor

Many thanks to Roy MacGregor and Kerry MacGregor for writing about this fantastic team of characters; Suzanne Sutherland, who brought everything together; Kelly Sonnack, my amazing agent; and my husband, Eric, for answering my many hockey questions.

—Kim Smith

ROY MACGREGOR, who was the media inductee into the Hockey Hall of Fame in 2012, has been described by the *Washington Post* as "the closest thing there is to a poet laureate of Canadian hockey." He is the author of the internationally successful Screech Owls hockey mystery series for young readers, which has sold more than two million copies and is also published in French, Chinese, Swedish, Finnish, and Czech. It is the most successful hockey series in history—and is second only to *Anne of Green Gables* as a Canadian book series for young readers—and, for two seasons, was a live-action hit on YTV. MacGregor has twice won the ACTRA Award for best television screenwriting.

KERRY MACGREGOR is co-author of the latest work in the Screech Owls series. She has worked in news and current affairs at the CBC, and as a journalist with the *Toronto Star*, the *Ottawa Citizen*, and many other publications. Her columns on parenting, written with a unique, modern perspective on the issues and interests of today's parents, have appeared in such publications as *Parenting Times Magazine*.

KIM SMITH is an illustrator from Calgary. She has illustrated several children's books including *The Great Puppy Invasion* and storybook adaptations of *Home Alone*, *The X-Files*, and *E. T. the Extra-Terrestrial*. Her favourite hockey team is the Calgary Flames. Go Flames, Go!